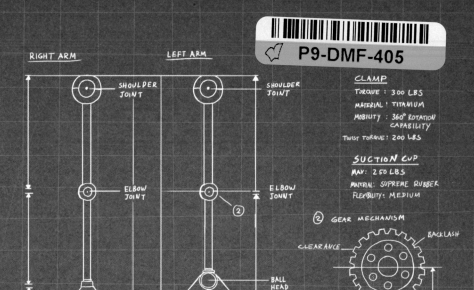

RIGHT ARM   LEFT ARM

SHOULDER JOINT

SHOULDER JOINT

② ELBOW JOINT

ELBOW JOINT

BALL HEAD

TITANIUM CLAMP

SUCTION CUP

CLAMP
TORQUE : 300 LBS
MATERIAL : TITANIUM
MOBILITY : 360° ROTATION CAPABILITY
TWIST TORQUE: 200 LBS

SUCTION CUP
MAX: 250 LBS
MATERIAL: SUPREME RUBBER
FLEXIBILITY: MEDIUM

② GEAR MECHANISM

BACKLASH

CLEARANCE

4

2.5'

3'

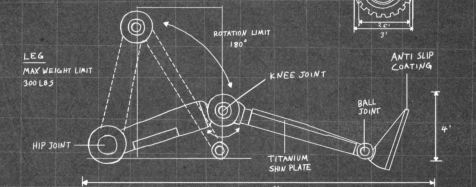

LEG
MAX WEIGHT LIMIT
300 LBS

ROTATION LIMIT 180°

KNEE JOINT

ANTI SLIP COATING

BALL JOINT

HIP JOINT

TITANIUM SHIN PLATE

4'

9'

GEAR SPECIFICATIONS

- 3.7 TURNS TO THE INCH IN HIGH GEAR

- 27.3 TURNS TO THE INCH IN LOW GEAR

- UNIVERSAL MOUNT FOR EACH JOINT

GEAR RATIO	A1	A2	B1	B2
VECTOR 5134 (229°)	30%	44.7%	50%	81.2%
TT-56 (306°)	2%	17%	18.2%	87.4%
DM-71H2 (16°)	—	5%	—	3.9%
GEAR RESISTANCE				
	R₁	R₂	R₃	R₄
TT-G6	141	251	184	176
DM-81-T4	132	267	175	8.6

GEAR RATIO	A1	A2	B1	B2
VECTOR 5134 (229°)	30%	44.7%	50%	81.2%
TT-56 (306°)	2%	17%	18.2%	87.4%
DM-71H2 (16°)	—	5%	—	3.9%

Gear resistance table:

	R_1	R_2	R_3	R_4
TT-G6	141	251	184	176
DM-81-T4	132	267	175	8.6

ARM

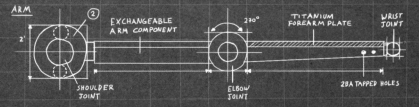

② EXCHANGEABLE ARM COMPONENT

270°

TITANIUM FOREARM PLATE

WRIST JOINT

2'

SHOULDER JOINT

ELBOW JOINT

2BA TAPPED HOLES

ROBOTS RULE!

LOTS
OF
BOTS

ROBOTS RULE!

LOTS OF BOTS

C. J. Richards

Illustrated by Goro Fujita

Houghton Mifflin Harcourt
Boston   New York

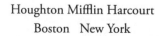

With special thanks to Brandon Robshaw

www.hmhco.com

Text set in Adobe Garamond

Library of Congress Cataloging-in-Publication Data is on file.

ISBN: 978-0-544-33934-7

Manufactured in the United States of America
DOC 10 9 8 7 6 5 4 3 2 1
4500527467

For James and Fiona McLaughlin

The pickup truck lurched sideways as Uncle Otto jerked the wheel, throwing George against the door.

"Out of the way, you metal moron!" Otto yelled, as they narrowly missed a mail-bot on the sidewalk.

"Look out!" George shouted. A robot-driven bus was heading straight toward them, its electronic horn blaring.

Otto braked hard with a screech of rubber, then swerved the truck back into its lane.

"That was close!" George said from the passenger seat, his heart pounding.

"Lucky for us I have good reflexes," Otto said. He was wearing his usual dingy work shirt and jeans, which

were dotted with engine-oil stains. "With all these robot drivers nowadays, sometimes I feel like I'm the only one on the road with a real brain in my head."

"Yes, an archaic one," muttered George's personal robot, Jackbot, from the backseat. "Obsolete, outdated, old-school."

George snorted a laugh.

"What was that, tin man?" growled Otto.

"Nothing," George said quickly. If Otto and Jackbot started going at it, they'd never get where they were going. "But have you ever considered that maybe it's time we got a smartcar too? Everyone else has one."

Otto gripped the steering wheel until his knuckles went white. "You think I'd let a bunch of wires and batteries drive me around?" he said. "Ha! Not in a million years. Trust me, George. Robots aren't the answer to every problem. I remember the days before all these tech geeks showed up—back when Terabyte Heights was just a little town called Termite Heights. Everything was so peaceful then . . ."

As Otto droned on about the joys of pre-robot life,

George stared out the window and watched the town flash by. Goosebumps rose along his arms as he realized they were nearly at TinkerTech Headquarters. It was the first day of George's apprenticeship, and he still couldn't quite believe it was happening. All his life he'd dreamed of working in the cutting-edge robotics workshop there, and today his dream was coming true. He'd be partnering with the greatest technological minds in the country, helping design robots that could think for themselves—just like he had with Jackbot.

Plus, he'd be away from school for a while, which meant no more run-ins with his enemy Patricia Volt and her league of supersnobs. She'd never quite forgiven him for driving the garbage truck that demolished her house, and George was convinced that she was still plotting revenge.

". . . Used to be you could take out your own trash without some recycling robot giving you a lecture," Otto was saying. "You could roast marshmallows on an open fire without one of those panicky metal fire marshals coming along with a fire extinguisher . . ."

A traffic-bot strode into the road ahead, holding out its metal hand. Its eyes flashed from green to yellow. But instead of slowing down, Otto pressed his foot on the gas and the truck sped forward.

"Um," said George, clutching his seat belt.

"I'm getting you to TinkerTech on time if it kills me!" Otto said.

"It might kill all of us!" Jackbot cried.

The traffic-bot leaped out of the way as they surged by, shouting "VIOLATION!" and spewing pink tickets from its mouth.

"Oh, relax, George," Otto said. "I haven't had one accident in thirty years."

"Well, there's a first time for everything," Jackbot said.

Thankfully, Otto did stop at the next light, but only because there was a traffic jam ahead and he didn't have much of a choice. George checked his watch. Despite scolding Otto for his dangerous driving, he *really* didn't want to be late. They were stopped next to a 3D hologram ad of a young woman in a business suit, with huge shiny eyes and a small white bud tucked into her ear. She beamed, displaying dazzling teeth, and said, "I'm connected. Are you?"

Next to her, a slogan hung in the air: "IT'S MODEST. IT'S MODERN. IT'S MOD™, TINKERTECH'S NEWEST INNOVATION. GET CONNECTED TODAY!"

"Wow," said George, staring dreamily at the ad. He'd been hearing about the MOD for months—maybe he'd get to try one out before it went on sale!

Otto shook his head dismissively. "Some new gizmo, huh?"

The traffic started rolling again. "Not just *any* new gizmo," said George. "It's probably the coolest thing since the *microchip*. MOD stands for Multifunctional Ocular Device—it's a wireless eye and earpiece combo that allows the wearer to access data just by thinking of it. It's like your *whole body* becomes one big computer, with your eyes as the screen and your brain—"

"My brain wouldn't touch that thing with a ten-foot

pole!" said Otto. "It would probably fry me like an egg. If you want a burnt-up brain, my boy, that's your choice —but you can leave me out of it."

Whatever his uncle's opinion on the topic, there was no way George was going to get left behind. He'd been saving from his weekend work at Otto's junkyard, and would be lining up with everyone else to buy his MOD in a few days.

How could he resist? The MOD was revolutionary. The user wore what appeared to be a special pair of contact lenses but was actually a tiny screen implanted with nanotech circuitry. With just the power of thought, information could either be displayed visually or relayed through the earpiece. It was the gadget to end all gadgets. And fried-egg brain or not, George was getting one.

A buzz came from George's pocket. He pulled out his battered old smartphone that Otto had finally gotten for him and saw a picture of Anne on the screen, with her white-blond hair and blue eyes. She was smiling and giving him a thumbs-up. "Knock 'em dead at TinkerTech, George!" the text underneath said. George smiled. Not only was it great to have a friend who wasn't composed of screws and bolts, but being pals with the daughter of Professor Droid, the president of TinkerTech, had its perks too.

"Thanks," George texted back. "I will!"

Finally, Otto pulled up to the soaring glass and steel offices of TinkerTech HQ—and not a moment too soon. The truck belched a cloud of black smoke, which drew hostile glances from the workers who were heading into the building. "Mark my words, George," said Otto. "The machines are taking over."

George sighed and unbuckled his seat belt. "Oh, don't be so paranoid," he said.

"You think I'm wrong?" said Otto. "You've got a short memory, then." He gave George a meaningful look.

George's smile faltered. Not so long ago, the machines nearly *had* taken over. The last deputy head of Robotics at TinkerTech, Dr. Charles Micron, had turned out to be a criminal mastermind, and nearly conquered Terabyte Heights with his army of bloodthirsty robots. Luckily George, with help from Jackbot and Anne, had managed to foil his evil plans. Micron had escaped, however, and hadn't been seen in Terabyte Heights since.

"Get in there and show those bots who's boss," Otto said, slapping George on the back.

"Thanks for the ride," said George, as he and Jackbot climbed out of the truck.

"And George!" Otto called through the open window. "Be careful, okay?"

"Sure," said George. He waved at his uncle as the beat-up truck pulled back into traffic, causing the blast of several horns. Otto might be a bit of a grouch, but

8

George knew deep down that his uncle cared for him. After all, he'd looked after George since the day his parents had died eight years ago. They'd been driving a smartcar that day. It had malfunctioned and careened over the edge of a cliff. Come to think of it, that was a pretty good reason to hate them.

"Earth to George—come in, George," said Jackbot, waving his pincer in front of George's face.

George blinked. "Oh—sorry," he said. "I was just thinking about my parents." He stared up at the gleaming tower. They'd once worked here too. Until recently George had thought they were just lowly file clerks, but now he wasn't so sure. He reached into his pocket for his lucky marble, a gift from his father just before the accident. George remembered that moment well—"Keep this safe, Georgie Porgie," his dad had said. "Keep it safe for your good old dad."

When George had first entered TinkerTech a few weeks ago, he'd thought that was all it was—a little souvenir of the parents he had lost. But now he knew differently. Inside TinkerTech the marble had glowed blue, and displayed a message within its swirling surface: "Project Mercury." George knew this was somehow connected with his parents, and he'd vowed to get to the bottom of the mystery. The problem was that the one person he thought could help him was not only his worst enemy, but also halfway across the world by now. Dr. Micron.

Jackbot rested his claw on George's shoulder. "Ready, amigo?"

George nodded and ran up the steps to the front doors, which were guarded by a very large robot dressed in a black military-style uniform. The robot had big square feet and a big square body and a big square head. They'd obviously improved security since all the trouble with Micron.

"Good morning," boomed the squares. "Identify yourselves, please."

"Hi. I'm George Gearing. I'm here to start the apprenticeship?"

"And I'm Jackbot. I'm here to keep him out of trouble."

The security-bot took a gleaming silver gun from its belt and pointed it straight at George's face.

"Hey!" said George, flinching. "What are you—?"

The robot waved the gun past George's eyes, but it only beeped. It wasn't a gun at all, he realized.

"Your iris pattern indicates that you are George Gearing," the robot stated, reholstering the device. "You may enter."

"Thanks," said George. He started to walk in with Jackbot, but the security-bot raised the scanner again, this time at Jackbot's head. George's personal bot rocked back on his heels.

"In case you haven't noticed, I don't have irises," he said.

"The scanner is now configured as a gun," said the security-bot. "Do not attempt to enter the premises or you will be annihilated."

"Charming," said Jackbot.

"No, wait," said George. "Jackbot is my personal bot. He's coming with me."

"Negative," said the security-bot. "Only authorized personnel may enter."

"But this place is *full* of robots!" said George. "*You're* a robot yourself!"

"I am an *authorized* robot," the security-bot said, and George was sure he detected a note of smugness in its voice.

He couldn't believe it. TinkerTech would be a giant pile of rubble if it hadn't been for Jackbot! George couldn't have defeated Micron without his help. George was about to argue with the security-bot, but Jackbot stopped him. "Go without me," he said. "You don't want to be late."

"But—"

"Go on," he said. "I'll be fine. I'll go read a book in the park or something."

George smiled sadly. Jackbot had already read thousands of books online. His processor was so powerful, it had only taken him about a day and a half. George thought his overuse of movie quotes was bad—but the random performances of Shakespearean monologues were worse.

"Look, I'll talk to Professor Droid," George said. "Get this sorted out. Stay close."

He left his friend and hurried through the front doors into the atrium. When he cast a look back, Jackbot was standing with his head hung low.

George took a deep breath and tried to focus on the moment. He was finally here. TinkerTech! And this time, he wasn't being arrested or chased by homicidal robots! He took in the gleaming glass and steel walls, the scientists in their crisp, white lab coats, and the sounds of bleeping, clicking robots—and sighed with happiness. He was so busy enjoying his surroundings that he wasn't looking where he was going, and walked right into someone. "Oof!" he said, and landed on his backside. A pocket tablet landed next to him with a crash.

"Omigosh," George gasped. "I'm so sorry!"

"Young man, watch where you're— Oh, George, it's you."

George looked up to see a tall, silver-haired man standing before him. It was Professor Droid—Anne's father and the founder of TinkerTech. He was the reason George had the apprenticeship in the first place. George and his friends had saved his life after Dr. Micron kidnapped him—and Droid was so grateful that he had rewarded George with the apprenticeship.

Droid didn't look so grateful now, though. His expression was stern, and the crowd of scientists behind him all stopped and stared at George like he was some kind of contagious computer virus.

George felt a blush rise to his cheeks. He picked up the smart tablet, noting with horror the spider web of cracks across its screen. "I—I think it might be broken."

Professor Droid looked at George as if not really seeing him. "Don't worry about it," he said, taking the tablet back from him.

George realized this wasn't the best time to bring up Jackbot's security clearance, but he might not get another chance.

"Professor, if you could spare . . ."

"Sir," interrupted a white-coated man. "As I was saying about the bug. It's almost impossible to identify—"

Droid held up a hand to silence the scientist. "Enough excuses!" he said. "The MOD launch is in three! Days'! Time!" His voice was rising in volume, and he punctuated each word with a stab of his finger. "If it doesn't happen, our share price will continue to plummet and the reputation of TinkerTech may never recover. You know how nervous the investors have been since that whole Micron disaster! *We need this project to be an unqualified success.* Do you understand me? So do your jobs, find the bugs, and *squish them.*" The scientists were trembling as Professor Droid finished his speech. George had never seen him angry before, and he realized for the first time how stressful it must be to run a business like TinkerTech. It wasn't all simply playing with circuits and developing cutting-edge technology.

The professor strode away without a backward glance, his gaggle of helpers trailing behind him.

George wandered toward the reception desk. Usually, the atrium of TinkerTech would be buzzing with robotic birds, but now there were lots of construction workers on scaffolding, still repairing the damage that Micron and his evil robot, the Caretaker, had caused.

The robotic receptionist watched with a cold smile as George approached. He shuddered. The last time George had seen her, she had been under Micron's control, and had tried to kill him with a stiletto heel. Thankfully, this time she seemed to be working perfectly on her own.

"Welcome to TinkerTech, Mr. Gearing," she said smoothly. George stood a little straighter. He wasn't used to being addressed in such a grown-up way. "If you take that elevator to the fifteenth floor"—she pointed with an elegant robot finger across the atrium—"your mentor will greet you."

"Thank you very much," George said.

As he waited for the elevator to arrive, George wondered who his mentor would be. He had hoped to work directly for Professor Droid, but that obviously wasn't going to be the case. He tried not to let disappointment get the better of him. There were plenty of other robotics whizzes at TinkerTech, and he was sure to learn something from whoever was training him.

The elevator doors opened. It was empty. "Hello, George!" said a bubbly voice. "Come on in!"

George did so, with another tickle of unease. Even the elevators had tried to murder him the last time he was here. "Fifteenth floor, please," he said.

"Well, sure thing, old buddy!" the elevator replied. The doors closed and it began to rise. "Lovely weather we're having," the elevator said after a moment.

"You think so?" said George, surprised. "It's kind of overcast today."

He watched the floors change. *Four . . . Five . . . Six . . .*

"Oh, I like clouds, don't you? They look like puffy little lambs in the sky!"

"They're all right, I guess," George said, thinking that whoever had programmed this elevator had gone a little overboard with the personality chip. George almost would have preferred the psychotic one.

"Oh, pooh!" the elevator said. "Another gloomy apprentice! She didn't appreciate the pretty clouds either."

George blinked. "Hold on. What other apprentice?" He'd assumed he was the only one.

"Well, we're here, Mr. Party Pooper," said the elevator, ignoring his question. *"Ping!"*

The doors slid open and George's heart sank to his knees.

Because there, dressed in an electric blue business suit and tapping at a smartphone, was Patricia Volt.

2

"**Well, well, well,**" **said Patricia, putting on a fake** smile. "If it isn't George Gearing. Fancy meeting *you* here." Next to her chair, a sleek silvery robot hovered in the air. It was about two feet long and was shaped like an oversized chess piece, with no limbs that George could see. It stared at him with blue, unblinking LED eyes.

"You . . . *you're* the other apprentice?" George stammered.

Patricia's smile vanished. "I am," she said. "Aren't you happy to see me?"

"But—I didn't think you were interested in robotics!"

Patricia smirked. "I am interested in anything that gets me out of school," she said. "Isn't that right, Cookie?"

"This boy's hygiene is unsatisfactory," announced the

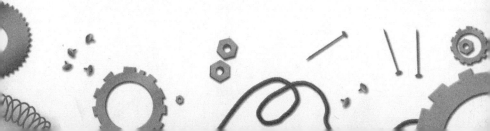

robot. "His sneakers are dirty, his T-shirt is wrinkled, and his hair is approximately an inch longer than optimum length. I calculate in three days he will acquire a zit on the right side of his nose due to oil overproduction. Makeover will commence in thirty seconds."

"Um, no, thanks," said George. "What is that thing, anyway?"

"This is Cookie," Patricia explained. "She's a meBot

series three—state of the art, of course. All the celebs have them now. She's a qualified hairstylist"—a panel opened in Cookie's sides and three pairs of scissors extended, snapping at the air—"a beauty expert"—lipsticks and brushes emerged—"and a nutritionist, yoga instructor, and personal shopper all in one." As soon as Patricia stopped speaking, all of the implements vanished silently back inside Cookie's metal figure.

"Oh, is that all?" said George, trying not to look impressed.

"No," Cookie said, before Patricia could answer, "I am also fluent in thirty languages, can perform advanced calculus, and am certified to repair a wide variety of home appliances."

This time, George couldn't hide his admiration. "Wow," he breathed. "Cool."

Patricia just looked bored.

"Do you think I could take a look at her CPU?" George asked, taking a step toward Cookie.

"Warning!" Cookie shouted, as an arm holding a

tiny spray bottle emerged from her frame. "If you touch me with those filthy hands I will be forced to sanitize you!"

George drew back, looking at his hands. "But they're clean," he said.

"'Clean' is a relative term," said the robot. "When was the last time you had a manicure?"

Ping! The elevator doors opened again, and Jackbot trundled out. "Have a super-duper day, little dude!" the elevator sang.

"Back at you, big guy!" Jackbot said.

"Jackbot!" said George, delighted to see his friend. "How did you get past the security-bot?"

"I told it I am your personal medical-bot."

"What do you mean?" George said. "Why would I need a doctor?"

"Oh, I just said you were suffering from some kind of post-traumatic stress disorder after you nearly got killed by Dr. Micron. That was clever, wasn't it? I mean, what harm could possibly come from—Oh!" Jackbot stopped dead, his eyes locked on Cookie.

"Hey . . . Jackbot," George said after a moment. "Are your batteries acting up again?"

"My whaaaa . . . ?" Jackbot mumbled, not looking at him.

George was beginning to worry. Were Jackbot's speech processors compromised too?

Jackbot walked forward slowly, passing Patricia, who looked as confused as George did. Then Jackbot reached for Cookie's sanitizer attachment and held it. "Do you have a GPS program?" he asked dreamily. "Because I'm getting lost in your eyes!"

Cookie snatched her arm away and floated above Jackbot. "Is this droid malfunctioning?" she said.

"My heart is," Jackbot replied.

"You have no heart," said Patricia. "You're just a bunch of circuits and scrap metal."

"Jackbot?" said George. "Maybe you should step back."

Jackbot didn't move. He just kept staring at the robot, the lights in his eyes flickering.

"George, can you please tell your robot to stop

flirting with *my robot?*" Patricia said. "She's way out of his league!"

George bristled. He had to admit that shabby little Jackbot looked pretty silly next to Cookie, but that wasn't the point. "He's the most intelligent robot in Terabyte Heights!" he said.

"More like the most intelligent trash can in Terabyte Heights," Patricia grumbled.

Jackbot slowly backed off to stand beside George. "She's the most beautiful bot I've ever seen," he whispered. "George, is this what love feels like?"

"I don't know," said George. "How does it feel?"

"Like my transistors are all firing at once," he said.

"Well," said George. "I guess either it's love or your CPU needs an upgrade."

At that moment, the door at the end of the hall opened and a man walked out. He wore a sharp suit and his face had a deep orange tan. As he approached, George was able to read the name tag on his lapel.

MAXIMILIAN VOLT, HEAD OF MARKETING.

So that's *how Patricia got this apprenticeship*, George mused.

"Welcome to TinkerTech, you two," he said. "I'll be your mentor throughout the program."

"Hi, Dad!" said Patricia.

Volt kissed his daughter. "Good to have you aboard, Sweetpea," he said. "This is going to be a lot of fun."

Then he turned to George. His mouth was still smiling, but his eyes weren't. "George Gearing, correct? You work hard and do what you're told and we'll get along just fine."

"Hey," said Jackbot, "aren't you going to kiss George, too?"

Volt narrowed his eyes and jerked a thumb at Jackbot. "Is this robot trying to be funny?"

"Um . . . yes," said George. "He does that."

"He shouldn't," said Volt. "Come on. We'll start with a tour."

As they walked down the corridor, George put his hand in his pocket and touched the blue marble. Okay, so this experience hadn't started in quite the way he had imagined, but it was still a huge opportunity. He wasn't going to let a little thing like Patricia Volt take that away from him. Jackbot tapped George on the shoulder.

"What's that scent she's wearing?" he whispered.

"Who?" said George.

"Cookie," said Jackbot. "She smells like a summer meadow."

George sniffed, but he couldn't smell a thing. "It's probably some sort of coolant," he said.

"Ah, *coolant*." Jackbot swooned.

"First, we'll tour the labs where the MOD device is being produced," Volt was saying. "This is going to be the biggest launch in TinkerTech history. Our analysts say it will change the way we work — think — live!"

"That sounds wonderful, Daddy," said Patricia. "Have you ordered one for me?"

"Of course I have, Sweetpea! For your mother, too. The whole town will be connected — well, ninety-eight percent of them, according to our projections."

"You think you'll be part of the two percent, George?"

said Patricia, casting a snide look at him. "Your tech isn't usually *cutting-edge*."

"Oh, I'll be getting one," George assured her.

They were marching down a long corridor with deep carpeting and walls that glowed with a creamy light. George had to trot to keep up; both Volt and his daughter walked with long, swift strides.

"The MOD will be the product of the century," Volt said. "Once everyone in Terabyte Heights is connected, we plan to roll it out across the country, and after that, the world!"

"Is everything all right with the launch?" George asked, about two paces behind. "I heard Professor Droid say something about bugs in the system."

Volt stopped. He looked down at George, his orange face stern. "The launch is going perfectly according to schedule, Mr. Gearing," he said. "You should keep your nose out of things that aren't your concern. Is that clear?"

Cookie suddenly spoke up. "Mr. Volt, your nose hair is approximately three centimeters too long. It's protruding from your nostrils in an unbecoming fashion.

27

Please prepare for corrective measures." An electric trimmer arm sprang from her body, and she advanced on Patricia's father.

"Get away from me!" said Volt, shielding his face. "Patricia, how many times do I have to tell you to keep that robot in check!"

"She cares about personal appearance," Patricia said. "She's just doing her job!"

"I'd let you trim my nose hair," Jackbot cooed, "if I had any hair . . . or a nose . . ."

Everyone ignored him.

Volt grumbled something under his breath and strode on. "Let's go."

They passed a door blocked by a metal barrier, with yellow tape crisscrossed over it that read CRIME SCENE — DO NOT ENTER.

"What's that?" asked George, pausing.

Volt stopped again. "That was the office of someone we prefer not to mention. He brought the whole company into disrepute, and I've had to do a *lot* of work to make people trust TinkerTech again."

"You mean Dr. Micron?" said George.

"Yes, the traitor!" Volt growled. "I always knew he was no good."

"I thought you used to go on fishing trips with him," Patricia piped up.

"Only to discuss business," Volt said, his jaw clenched.

"But what about all those dinner parties?" Patricia continued. "You used to call him Good Old Chip, remember?"

Volt twitched and cleared his throat. "My, look at the time," he said, glancing at his watch. "Hurry up, children. No time to waste."

Volt stalked off and George was about to follow when he felt a sudden warmth coming from his pocket. After making sure no one was looking, he pulled out the marble. It was glowing bright red.

He'd only seen the marble glow blue, never red. George looked from the marble to Micron's old office. Could it be that something in that room was triggering the marble's circuitry?

"Hey, Jackbot, check this out," he said.

Jackbot had been gazing after Cookie longingly, but now he turned his attention to the marble. He took it from George's hand and moved closer to the door. It glowed brighter and brighter like a miniature fireball.

"Weird," Jackbot said.

"Yeah," George agreed. He couldn't explain it, but without knowing for sure what the color change meant, he could swear the marble was trying to warn him about something. Dr. Micron had known his parents, that much he knew. Micron's parting words before escaping on the Caretaker had been that George was too clever for his own good—*just like his parents.* Those words had haunted him ever since. Why would an executive like Micron have even known his parents existed if they'd only been clerks? George had a feeling that there was more to the story.

George took a last look at the office door. "We've got to get inside," he whispered to Jackbot. "There's information about my parents in there, I just know it."

"Sounds dangerous, hazardous, and risky," said Jackbot. His eyes flashed. "I'm in!"

"Hey! Enough lollygagging, Mr. Gearing," called Maximilian Volt from farther down the corridor. "Let's go!"

George pocketed the marble and he and Jackbot jogged to catch up with Patricia and her father.

"Here we are," said Volt. "MOD Central Processing." They had reached a shiny steel wall that seemed like a dead end. But when Volt pressed his palm against it, a red light scanned his hand from top to bottom and then glowed blue. Suddenly the wall began to rise.

George caught his breath. "Whoa."

Beyond the wall was a metal bridge that spanned a manufacturing floor as long as a football field. Twenty feet below, a vast expanse of machinery hissed and beeped as a conveyor belt moved around the room in an endless loop. Robotic arms suctioned items off the belt and whizzed them over to other stations. Here and there showers of sparks flew into the air like tiny fireworks. Vats of chemicals covered with warning symbols lined one edge of the factory floor. At the far end of the room,

George saw people dressed head to toe in white sterile suits. Some were working at mobile computer panels while others hurried across bridges suspended over the machines. It was a crazy, noisy dance of machines and people. George thought it was absolutely fantastic.

"Quite something, isn't it?" said Volt, seeing the look of awe on George's face.

A robot that looked vaguely like a department store mannequin stood by the door next to a cart stacked with white bodysuits. George thought it was creepy-looking.

"Max Volt, Security Clearance Alpha," Volt said. "I'm here to give the apprentices a tour."

"Please wear a protective garment," said the robot, holding out an armful of the bodysuits. "Robots too."

"Do you have a choice of colors?" Cookie asked. "White is unsuited to my owner's complexion. Jade green would be sufficient, or burnt umber."

The robot blinked. "You will wear protective garments," it repeated.

"We're making lenses that go in people's eyes," said Volt, as they all pulled the suits over their clothes. "We can't take any risks with contamination."

Jackbot's suit was much too big for him and dragged on the floor. "How do I look, Cookie?" he asked, striking a pose.

Patricia's bot turned her gaze on him. "Very last season," she replied.

"Follow me!" said Volt.

The metal bridge clanked as they marched across it. George looked down at the scene below. The machinery was unexpectedly large, considering it was making tiny earpieces and lenses. A hose extended from one machine, dripping globules of a quivering translucent jelly onto the belt.

"What's that?" George said.

"That's what we make the lenses from," Volt explained. "A liquid polymer patented by TinkerTech. We treat it with high heat to form a malleable solid, then implant nanotech between its molecular layers." He chuckled. "That Micron was a crook, but he sure was a genius."

"Wait," said George. "Micron designed the MOD?"

"He did almost all of the initial design, yes," said Volt. "Though we don't like to advertise that."

I suppose I shouldn't be surprised, thought George. *Micron was deputy head of Robotics, after all.*

Volt looked thoughtful as he observed the activity. "Frankly, without Micron, the MOD never would have been invented. His technology was beyond even our best developers' expertise. We can build the things to his specifications, but there are parts of its mechanics that we still don't quite understand." Volt shook his head.

"It's really too bad Chip turned out to be a criminal mastermind."

For the first time, George agreed with Volt. Micron had once been George's idol—the man he had most wanted to be like when he grew up. Now that couldn't be further from the truth.

"So," Volt said, continuing the tour. "The polymer gets taken to the press first, over there." He pointed at a giant machine that slammed down an enormous hammer onto the pale jelly every few seconds. After it had been flattened, the jelly moved on, now paper thin and no longer quivering. "The width of the lens can be controlled within a picometer."

"A trillionth of a meter?" George exclaimed. "That's incredible."

He stood aside as a man came down the bridge, holding a pocket tablet and stabbing at the screen. The man wasn't really watching where he was going.

"What does that machine do?" Patricia asked. She pointed at something that looked like an upside-down hedgehog, which slammed down onto the flattened lens material as it passed by. George leaned over to look.

"That's the cutter," said Volt. "It carves the material into lenses. Then the laser implants the—"

Suddenly someone shoved George in the back. Hard.

His insides lurched with terror as he tipped head over heels off the bridge. Desperately, he flailed his arms as he fell, and he managed to catch the rail with one hand.

For a moment he hung by his fingertips, his feet kicking the air.

"George!" said Jackbot, leaping forward. He grabbed for George's hand, but it was too late.

George's fingers slipped off the rail, and he plummeted toward the conveyor belt below with a cry. *I'm dead I'm dead I'm dead!* George thought in the timeless moments as he fell. But instead of smashing against the hard concrete, George landed on top of the quivering gel, which softly buoyed him up like a liquid trampoline.

As he lay there flat on his back, miraculously still alive, George saw Volt, Patricia, Jackbot, Cookie, and a group of white-suited workers all staring down at him

in horror. "I'm okay!" George shouted. But for some reason, they didn't look reassured.

"Shut it down!" yelled Patricia's father to one of the workers on the floor.

"I don't have the security code!" the man replied.

"Really, I'm fine," George said, and tried to get up. But he couldn't move. He was stuck to the gel like a bug on flypaper. He quickly realized that the conveyor belt was moving. He craned his neck to see what was ahead.

He was being carried toward the stamping press.

"Who has the code?" shouted Volt. "Where's the foreman?"

"Coffee break!" said another worker.

THUD! The giant head of the hammer thundered down on the section of gel just ahead of George. His whole body vibrated with the force of it.

George tugged with all his might, but he couldn't move a limb. In another few seconds, he was about to find out just how thin a picometer really was.

3

THUD!

The hammer crashed down again. "Help!" George shouted. "Help me!"

"Do something!" he heard Volt yell. "Stop the machine!"

A high-pitched alarm cut through the air.

Panicked voices, running footsteps. "I can't override it!" someone shouted. "We'll never get into the program in time!"

THUD!

Next time it'll be me, George thought, writhing desperately.

He passed right beneath the shadow of the press. His stomach twisted with fear as its smooth black surface

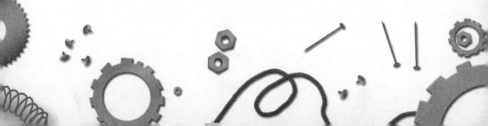

hovered above his head, hydraulics hissing. He wanted to look away but he couldn't. The hammer descended.

CCRRRARSSSSSQUESHKKKKK!

With a grinding, screeching noise, the hammer came to a stop about three inches from George's nose.

The conveyor belt juddered to a halt. Jackbot was suddenly at his side.

"Jackbot! How—?"

The robot brandished a handful of torn wires in his metal claw. "Manual override," he said.

Jackbot tugged George's arms, yanking him free of the sticky gel. The alarms cut out abruptly, leaving his ears ringing.

George fell off the conveyor belt and staggered to his feet, knees shaking.

Max Volt, followed by Patricia and Cookie, came running toward them. His face was like a thundercloud. An orange one.

"Are you out of your mind?" he shouted. "You could have been killed!"

"Don't worry. I'm fine," said Jackbot, polishing his

40

pincer on his chest plate. "It was nothing, really. All in a day's work."

"Not you!" said Volt. He jabbed a finger at George. "Him!"

"Yeah, George!" said Patricia. "How could you just fall off the bridge? I mean, what are you, three years old?"

"I didn't fall!" George spluttered. "Someone pushed me!"

"Oh, *please!*" said Patricia, crossing her arms. "Talk about attention seeking!"

"I swear," said George. "It was one of the workers. He was wearing a white suit."

Volt sucked in a breath. "That's a serious accusation, my boy," he said. "And it doesn't change the fact your robot just caused millions of dollars' worth of damage."

"He saved me!" said George. "That press would have flattened me like a pancake!"

"I could probably fix it," said Jackbot, holding up the wires hopefully. "If you just give me a screwdriver and some chewing gum—"

"No. You've done enough," said Volt. "I don't know how I'm going to explain this to . . ."

George heard someone walking toward them.

"What's happened here?" Professor Droid asked. "I heard the alarm. Why has production been interrupted?"

"George jumped on the conveyor belt!" Patricia said. "And then his robot trashed the squishing machine."

Droid's face cycled through a series of emotions: confusion, panic, anger.

"I'm okay," said George.

Droid flashed him a quick smile. "Good. Good," he

said, his voice controlled. "How long will it take to fix, Max?"

"We don't know yet," Volt said gravely. "I'll get the engineers on it right away, but—it doesn't look good."

"Could this jeopardize the launch?" asked Droid.

Volt looked grim. "If we don't get it fixed immediately, then yes. We've only produced fifty percent of the stock so far."

Droid bowed his head, then turned to George. "Not a great start to your apprenticeship, is it?" George didn't know what to say. Without any proof that he was pushed, he knew his claim sounded ridiculous.

"I put a lot of trust in you, George," Droid said. "Don't make me regret it."

George saw Patricia smirking. "I won't, sir," he said.

"I'm wondering if we should put him someplace where he can't do any more damage," Volt said. "He can still make himself useful, away from the sensitive areas. Since he seems to be a bit . . . unstable at the moment."

"Good thinking, Max," Droid said. "But where?"

Volt folded his arms, and George could have sworn he saw the ghost of a smile.

"How about Department Six?" he said.

"Where are we going? What's Department Six?" George asked for the third time.

Volt had remained silent from the moment they left the manufacturing floor until they reached the elevator. He instructed the elevator to take them to the basement.

"Very useful work," he said. "Vital for the smooth running of TinkerTech."

The elevator giggled.

"But I was just starting to get to know Cookie!" Jackbot whispered. "I don't like this at all."

George didn't like it either. He guessed it wasn't worth continuing to plead his innocence, so maybe it was time for a change in tactics.

"Look, Mr. Volt, we got off on the wrong foot. I know you're probably still upset about that accident at your house a couple of weeks ago."

Volt's smile was tight. "You mean when a rogue garbage truck-bot destroyed my home? That wasn't your fault either, I seem to recall."

George winced. "Yes . . . but, I really do know a lot about robotics. I swear! I could be very useful if you'd just give me a chance."

"Don't worry," said Volt. "You'll be working with a robot with *priority* access to all areas of the building."

Well, that doesn't sound too bad, George thought.

The elevator doors opened into a very large room with a stone floor, and shelves stacked with all manner of cans, bottles, boxes, brushes, brooms, mops, and buckets. "Here we are!" Volt said. "Department Six!"

They stepped out and the elevator doors swished shut behind them.

George scanned the room. "This looks a lot like a really big janitor's closet," he said.

He heard a humming noise and spun to his right. A robot so huge its head almost brushed the ceiling was rolling toward them. George's heart did a double somersault. *It can't be . . .*

The Caretaker. Micron's personal attack-bot—a powerful, unstoppable machine. It was coming right for him on tractor treads, its eyes flashing and hands bristling with tools.

George searched frantically for a weapon, and grabbed a mop. "Don't try anything," he shouted. "I'm armed!"

"Leave it to me!" said Jackbot. He ran across the room and launched a flying kung fu kick at the robot. There was a very loud *CLANG* and Jackbot bounced off the monster and landed on his head. "Ouch!" he said.

The robot, completely undisturbed, continued to advance on George.

"We have to get out of here, Mr. Volt!" George said, stumbling back toward the elevator. "That robot's dangerous!"

Volt laughed. "Don't worry, George. That's not the Caretaker. Same model, but a completely different central processing unit. We call it the Occupational Cleaning Droid—or the OCD-bot for short. It's not dangerous at all—except to dirt!"

"Dirt and germs I must destroy! Cleaning is my only joy!" said the OCD-bot in a high-pitched, singsong voice. It rolled to a halt in front of George. "In your hand you have a mop! Mop and mop until you drop!"

"We programmed it with a rhyming generator," Volt said. "Cute, huh? So, you just go along with the OCD-bot and it will explain all the tasks you'll be assigned."

George's fear gave way to disappointment. "Wait a minute," he said. "You're putting me on . . . *cleaning duty?*"

"You will find that cleaning duty has a special kind of beauty!" sang the OCD-bot.

"I'm a TinkerTech apprentice!" George said. "I'm supposed to be here to learn about robotics!"

"After your antics this morning, I think it's best for you to be on cleaning detail for a while," Volt said. "At least until after the MOD launch is over. You just concentrate on being the greatest cleaning assistant you can be, okay?" He gave George a sunny, white-toothed smile, turned around, and hit the elevator button. He was still smiling as the doors swished shut and the elevator carried him away.

"I can't believe this!" George said to Jackbot. "It's a total disaster."

"I know," Jackbot said, shaking his head in sorrow. "I'll hardly get to see Cookie at all."

"The first-floor passages are dusty!" said the OCD-bot. "Bring your mop, so true and trusty!" It started to roll toward the door.

"Do you *always* have to speak in rhyme?" George asked, as they followed the robot out.

"When I clean, I speak in rhyme," sang the OCD-bot, "and I'm cleaning all the time!"

This is going to be a long, long day, thought George.

• • •

For the rest of the morning, George and Jackbot assisted the OCD-bot in scrubbing floors, picking up litter, emptying trash cans, and vacuuming carpeted areas. The robot kept getting radio messages causing it to stop what it was doing, make a bleepy noise, and then announce things like: "We have to wash a dirty door! It's on the twenty-seventh floor!"

By lunchtime, George was exhausted. His back was aching, his nostrils were filled with the scent of cleaning products, and he felt like he hadn't eaten in a week. "Don't we get a break?" he asked the OCD-bot, as they were polishing furniture in the boardroom.

"I never, ever have a break," said the OCD-bot. "A break's a thing I do not take!"

"A break is something bots don't require," Jackbot said. "But boys like George will sometimes tire."

"Thanks, Jackbot," George said.

The OCD-bot suddenly stopped squirting polish on the boardroom table and bleeped again. "Emergency, emergency!" it sang. "We must respond with urgency!"

George sighed. "What happened now?"

"A donut-bot has gone berserk! Necessitating extra work!"

"A donut-bot?" said George, suddenly feeling even hungrier.

"It's in the Records Office, yes. Creating a tremendous mess!" said the OCD-bot.

The Records Office, George thought. *I could dig around for information about my mom and dad!*

"Leave it to us," he told the OCD-bot. "Jackbot and I will take care of it. What floor's it on?"

"The seventh floor is the location of this messy situation!" OCD-bot sang.

"Let's go!" said George, and he and Jackbot ran from the room.

The seventh floor looked like a scene from the world's biggest food fight. A group of workers cowered in the corridor, their clothes and faces spattered all over with bits of donut, frosting, and filling. One man was lying on his back as an older woman slapped his face to rouse him.

"Is he okay?" asked George.

"Just shock, we think," the woman said. She had a smear of chocolate frosting across her face and multicolored sprinkles scattered in her graying hair. "He put in his usual request for a bear claw and the donut-bot spun him around in his chair and stuffed a donut hole in each ear. He fainted, the poor thing."

"We had to evacuate the Records Office!" added a man with strawberry jelly all over his suit. "I'm nursing a second-degree burn because of that thing! Someone has to go and switch it off!"

"Leave it to us," George announced, brandishing his mop.

"It's in there," said a man, pointing with a trembling hand toward a door that was barricaded with a filing cabinet. Even as George watched, a hail of donuts splattered against the glass panel. "But be careful!"

"This will be a piece of cake!" Jackbot said. He looked around expectantly. "Get it? Cake?" Everyone just stared at him. "Boy, tough crowd."

"Come on!" George said, pulling him away. George

peered through the panel in the door, but couldn't see much past the caramel sauce smears. He put his shoulder against the filing cabinet, shoved it aside, and placed his hand on the doorknob.

"Ready?" he said to Jackbot.

Jackbot nodded. "Let's do this."

George eased open the door, staying low. He couldn't see the bot between the office cubicles. Come to think of it, he didn't even know what a donut-bot looked like. He turned to Jackbot and pointed left. "You go that way!" he whispered.

Jackbot took one step and his foot squelched in a puddle of cream. Across the office came a series of clicks and beeps.

"Incoming!" shouted Jackbot.

The first donut whistled past George's ear and smashed into the wall behind him. The second caught his shoulder and burst into a shower of jam and powdered sugar. Then Jackbot leaped onto George, forcing him down to the floor and out of the line of fire.

"Come and get your piping hot donuts! Yum, yum, yum!" shouted a rough voice.

George and Jackbot scrambled to their knees and hid under a desk as the pastry bombardment continued. George was breathing hard. He peeked over the edge of the desk and got a first glimpse of their enemy—a short, fat robot with a round head and a big, clownlike smile. Its head rotated 360 degrees, searching for them with unblinking eyes.

"You're hit," said Jackbot, pointing to George's shoulder.

George swiped the red sauce with his finger and tasted it. "It's only raspberry. He must have an Off switch. C'mon. I'll draw his fire. You sneak up from behind."

"No," said Jackbot. "It's too risky. I'll be the decoy."

Before George could argue, Jackbot jumped up. "Over here!" he shouted.

Two donuts hit him in the face, blinding him. Then a blur of projectiles drove him back. Jackbot staggered and slid across the ground, lying completely still.

"Jackbot!" George shouted.

His friend held out a spindly arm. "Leave me, George!" he gasped. "I think I'm done for."

George grabbed a notebook off a nearby table and ran to his friend. The sugary barrage recommenced at once, but George shielded himself with the binder. He seized Jackbot's arm and tugged him to safety behind a cupboard. Wiping the jam and cream off Jackbot's face, he asked, "Are you okay?"

"I guess I'll live."

"I got plenty more where that came from!" called the bot. "Who wants donuts? They're hot, hot, hot!"

George risked a glance and saw the robot trundling toward them, steaming donuts launching from its hand like grenades.

The mop was lying on the ground between them. "Stay here," George said to his friend. "I've got an idea."

Gritting his teeth, George pushed himself into a commando roll across the ground, snatching up the mop as he went. The donuts started flying immediately. George sprang up and brought the mop down in a vertical swipe. The bot's arm detached from its body, hitting the ground with a clang. George ducked as the remaining arm flung more treats at an astonishing rate. He covered the bot's face with the dirty mop head, blinding its visual sensors. Where was the Off switch?

Just then Jackbot sprang from his hiding spot and hurled himself at the bot's remaining arm, hanging from it like a monkey.

"Please do not interfere with this robot," said an automated voice. "Tampering with DonutKing property may result in a fine."

The bot struggled and spun on the spot. Jackbot held on for dear life as its mouth opened, spraying chocolate sprinkles in a blinding hailstorm across the office. George suddenly spied a red button at the base of its neck.

"Hurry, George!" shouted Jackbot as his body whizzed through the air. "I can't hold on much longer!"

George vaulted onto a desk to avoid a squirt of fudge sauce and a blizzard of marshmallows that were now shooting from the bot's mouth. Trying to get the timing right, he watched the bot spinning . . . and then kicked his heel onto the switch. At the same moment, Jackbot lost his grip, hurtled over a computer monitor across the room, and landed with a crunch.

"Wurrrrgh," said the donut-bot. "I'm sorry, we are all out of donutssssssss-*click*." The light went out of its eyes and it stopped moving, dropping a final donut onto the floor with a splat.

Jackbot emerged from the other side of the office, rolling his neck back and forth. "I think I have chocolate cream in my circuits," he said. "It's kind of nice."

George surveyed the damage. Just about every available surface was covered with donut debris—including the ceiling. He held out the mop to Jackbot. "You'd better get started. Seal off the room."

"Me?" Jackbot said. "What about you?"

"I have some research to do," George said. It was too good a chance to miss. He swept a pile of donuts off a chair, sat at a computer, and, taking one of the sponges the OCD-bot had given him out of his back pocket, wiped the cream off the monitor. While he got started, Jackbot explained to the office workers that the cleanup would take some time, and that they should all probably go have a shower in the locker rooms.

George was happy to finally be in his element. He had no problem accessing the system—the workers had fled the office in such a hurry that they had forgotten to log out of their accounts. He quickly located the staff records search, and typed in the dates he guessed his parents had worked for TinkerTech. A huge list of names appeared on the screen. George scrolled down to the Gs: Ganzer, Garbonanza, Garfield, Gatling, Gatsby, Gax, Geables, Geach, Gillibrow . . .

George was confused. There was nothing between Geach and Gillibrow. No Gearing.

He tried a year earlier. Same result. A year before that and still no Gearing. He scrolled back five years, then forward eight, and still . . . No record of his parents whatsoever.

"This is weird," George said to Jackbot, who had already finished cleaning up most of the mess. "My mom and dad used to work here. I know they did. Otto said so, and Dr. Micron too. But they're not on the system!"

"That *is* weird," Jackbot said. "Bizarre, mysterious, peculiar."

I need to dig deeper, thought George. *But where else can I look?*

Jackbot's eyes flashed. "Sorry, George. Incoming call from the OCD-bot."

"What does he say?" asked George.

Jackbot took on the cleaning bot's voice.

"A bathroom drain is on the blink—bring your mask, there's quite a stink!"

George sighed.

So the long day wore on. All through the afternoon, as George scrubbed and polished and tidied, a question kept nagging at his mind: *Why weren't Mom and Dad on the system?* Otto had no reason to lie to him about it. And Micron knew them, so they must have been at TinkerTech. It was as if someone had erased them from the company's history.

George was tempted to go straight to Professor Droid, but the OCD-bot barely gave them a chance to breathe all afternoon. And anyway, after the disaster on the MOD manufacturing floor, George was pretty sure Droid wouldn't give him the time of day.

Finally it was five o'clock, and George switched off the vacuum cleaner with relief.

"It's bye for now, but feel no sorrow," said the OCD-bot. "More dirt and dust to clean tomorrow!"

"Can't wait," mumbled George.

The elevator returned George and Jackbot to the ground floor. "Have a totally fantastic day!" it said cheerfully.

They walked to the bus stop outside the TinkerTech building. Otto had told George he wouldn't be there to pick him up — he was working late at the junkyard, as usual.

"What a day," George said.

"Yes, it was!" Jackbot said dreamily. "I met the most beautiful robot in all the world. I think I'm in love!"

"You can't really be in love," George said. "You're a robot."

"So?" said Jackbot. "Do you think that because I'm a robot I have no heart?"

"I *know* you have no heart," said George. "I built you."

"Well, I have a lithium battery," said Jackbot proudly. "And it's filled with love for Cookie! Tell me, George — how can I prove my love to her?"

"I don't know," George said. "Can't you look it up? There's all kinds of books about that sort of thing. Dating tips, relationship advice, romance how-to's. I'm sure you could download an entire love library if you really wanted to."

"That's a great idea, George!" Jackbot said. "I'm going to become an expert on love!"

The robot-driven bus appeared and pulled up in front of them. It was crowded with people heading home after a hard day's work. As George squeezed on with Jackbot, he heard snatches of conversation.

"Have you ordered yours yet?"

"Oh yes! I've ordered sets for the kids, too."

"Of course, it would be awful if they were the only ones without it."

"Gotta keep up with the times!"

George managed a smile. It looked like the TinkerTech analysts were right—*everyone* wanted to own a MOD. Micron would be proud his invention was so popular.

Wherever he was lurking.

The thought made George shudder. Something told him that he hadn't seen the last of Dr. Micron.

"It'll be like having an extra brain!" said a passenger next to George.

"There sure is a lot riding on this," George whispered to Jackbot.

"What?" said Jackbot. He'd been downloading files; George could tell by the faraway look in his eyes. "Oh, I know. If I can just impress Cookie . . ."

"I meant the MOD launch," said George.

Jackbot nodded absently. "You know, I've just processed every known text referencing love and I've come to a conclusion."

"Which is?"

"Love is confusing," said Jackbot. "For instance, according to more than one source, love makes the world go round." Jackbot cocked his head. "But that's not true. The world goes round because of angular momentum."

"It's just an expression," George said.

"People should say what they mean!" said Jackbot. "Anyway, another book said you can write poetry and send it to the loved one. I'm going to try that, George. I'm going to write love poetry!"

"Well, I hope you're a better poet than the OCD-bot," George said. "Come on, this is our stop."

When they got home, there was loud music coming from the living room. George frowned. What was going on in there? He opened the front door to find Otto, with the radio on, sitting comfortably in an armchair and drinking a large mug of coffee. A half-eaten hamburger and a pile of steaming french fries sat on a plate by his side.

"Hey, Otto," said George, surprised. "You're home early!"

"I certainly am," Otto said, beaming.

George hadn't seen him smile like that for a long time. Well, *ever*. "You're . . . in a good mood."

"Yes, indeedy!" said Otto.

"Are you in love?" asked Jackbot.

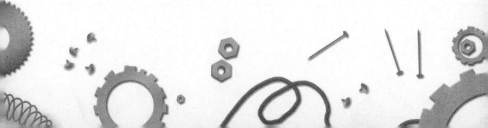

Otto laughed. "No, I'm not in love—except with life! Had a real good piece of news today."

"What happened?" George asked.

"Someone offered to buy my junkyard!" Otto said. "For a *lot* of money. We're talking big bucks!" He stood up and grabbed George by the shoulders. "You hear that, kid? We're rich!"

"Rich?" said George, mystified. "But the junkyard can't be worth that much, can it? The whole place is falling to pieces, and it's in a rundown part of town—"

"Someone spotted its potential," said Otto, getting up and starting to dance around the room to the music, to George's astonishment. "This lawyer type came into the yard today and said he represents a client who wants to buy the land. Made me an offer right then and there! It's going to change our lives, George! No more hand-me-down robots for you!"

"I beg your pardon!" Jackbot said.

"Well, except for you, Jackbot," Otto replied.

George didn't know what to say. "That sounds . . . great!" he finally managed.

"So, how was your first day at TinkerTech?" Otto asked.

"Eventful," George said.

"It was life-changing!" said Jackbot.

"What's with him?" asked Otto, jerking his thumb at Jackbot.

"He thinks he's in love."

"I *am* in love!" said Jackbot. "With the most beautiful robot in the world!"

Otto laughed. "Now I've heard it all. The juicer's got a crush on me too." He laughed at his own joke.

"Otto," George said. He sat, and his uncle returned to his easy chair. "Can I ask you something?"

"Ask away," said Otto, stuffing a couple of fries into his mouth.

"Mom and Dad — they used to work at TinkerTech, right?"

Otto stopped chewing and swallowed hard. "Um, that's right. I think they did."

"You *think?*" repeated George. "Or you know?"

Otto looked uncomfortable. "I'm pretty sure. I mean — yes, they did. They worked there."

"And when was that, exactly?" asked George.

"A long time ago," Otto said, sighing.

"But can't you remember exactly? I looked them up at TinkerTech today—and there's no record of them. How could that be, if they really did work there?"

"No idea," Otto said. "It's a mystery. You'll find life's full of mysteries as you get older, George, and some of them just can't be solved. Put it out of your mind, boy. Here, have a french fry."

George was about to argue, but he was interrupted by a knock on the door.

"I'll get it!" said Jackbot. "It might be Cookie!"

It wasn't. Jackbot returned with Anne and her robot dog, Sparky.

"Anne!" George said, jumping up from his chair. "I'm so glad you're here!"

"Yes, as am I!" Jackbot chimed in. He clasped Anne's hand in his pincer, and stared directly into her eyes. "'Shall I compare thee to a summer's day?'"

Anne snorted. "What's with you?"

"No, I can't, because 'Thou art more lovely and more temperate.'" Jackbot contrived.

"I think your robot's gone off the rails again," Anne whispered to George.

"That was a bit of Shakespeare," Jackbot said. "One of his sonnets. Do you feel like running away with me now?"

Anne's eyebrows rose. "I do feel like running away, but *from* you, not *with*—"

"See?" Jackbot hissed to George, interrupting her. "I think this is going to work! All I have to do is write a love poem telling Cookie how I feel, and she'll fall head over heels for me!"

Anne gave George a questioning look, and he shook his head. "I'll explain later," he said.

"Have a fry!" said Otto, offering Anne the plate. "Have a whole plate of them! After today, I can afford to buy all the fries in town!"

"Really?" asked Anne, taking a handful. "What happened?"

"Someone bought my junkyard! For a whole truck-load of cash!"

"Wow," Anne said, munching. "I just came by to see what happened on George's first day."

George hesitated. If he said that Professor Droid had ignored him and allowed him to be demoted to cleaning assistant, it would sound like he was complaining about her dad. "It was great," he said. "Just great."

"I knew you'd love it!" Anne said. "Anyway, my dad's having a barbecue this weekend to celebrate the MOD launch, and I thought you and Jackbot might like to come."

At last, something good was happening today! "We'd love to!" said George.

"A barbecue, eh?" said Otto, sitting up straighter. Out of his uncle's eyeline, George shook his head vigorously. There was no way his uncle would fit in.

"You can come too if you like," Anne said politely.

George sighed.

"Thanks. I will!" Otto said.

"You know it'll be full of techy people, don't you?"

George said. "All those nerds from TinkerTech, talking about boring robots and things."

"So?" Otto asked. "I can hold my own with those big shots! I'm the best mechanic in town!"

"Will Cookie be there?" asked Jackbot.

"Who is Cookie?" said Anne.

"The most beautiful robot in the world," said Jackbot dreamily.

"Is Patricia Volt invited?" said George.

Anne nodded. "The Volts are pretty important at TinkerTech."

"Then Cookie will be there too," said George. "She's Patricia's new personal bot."

Otto stood up, spilling crumbs on the floor. "I think I'll buy myself a new outfit. Now that I've sold the yard, I can get myself a whole new wardrobe!"

That reminded George of something he'd been meaning to ask. "What's going to happen to all the stuff in the junkyard?"

"Not my problem," Otto said, shrugging. "The new guy's going to get rid of it, I guess."

A wave of sadness hit George. He'd spent countless days at the junkyard in the past, tinkering with circuitry and searching for parts. His uncle's junk pile was George's gold mine, and it hurt him to think it would be gone forever. After all, Jackbot was built almost entirely out of scrap from that yard.

"Do you mind if I go and have a look around?" George asked. "See if there's anything worth saving?"

"Sure, go nuts," Otto said, tossing a big jangling bunch of keys over his shoulder. They hit Jackbot on the head. "I gave the new owner my keys, but I always keep a spare or two handy."

"Gee, thanks," said Jackbot.

"Do you want to come?" George asked Anne.

"Yeah, we'll come. Won't we, boy?" said Anne. The electronic dog barked, then farted. "Sparky!" said Anne. "Manners!"

"I'd rather stay here, if that's okay with you, George," Jackbot said. "I want to work on my poem for Cookie. I wish her name were easier to rhyme, though. If only she'd been called Sue! 'Sue, Sue, I love you true . . .'"

"So, what exactly is wrong with him?" Anne asked when Jackbot was out of sight.

"Long story," George said.

Dusk was falling by the time they reached the junkyard. Masses of black clouds rolled in the darkening sky, and lonesome crows cawed from the bare branches of trees. The temperature had dropped by several degrees, and George shivered as he fumbled with the padlock on the tall, rusty gate. Behind the chainlink fence, junk was stacked up in high, teetering piles that in the twilight looked like massive monster robots. Towering over everything was a crane with a giant magnet, used for lifting and moving broken-down cars. It looked like a metallic dinosaur.

"Kind of spooky, isn't it?" Anne said, looking around nervously.

George knew what she meant, but didn't admit it. "There's nothing to worry about," he said, keeping his voice light. "No one's here except us."

The padlock opened at last. "After you!" said George.

"No, after *you*," said Anne.

The yard was filled with ancient, rusting cars, motorbikes, fridges, stoves, lawnmowers, washing machines, towers of defunct computers, and various twisted bits of metal that even George didn't recognize. Over the years, as Terabyte Heights had slowly become more and more robotic, Otto's Grotto was the place where old appliances came to die.

"Wow!" said Anne. "This place is a real *dump!*"

"I guess," George said, feeling suddenly defensive.

"I mean, a really cool dump . . ." Anne added, after seeing the look on George's face.

George stared at the junkyard with affection. After the disastrous day at TinkerTech, it felt good to be back in familiar surroundings. After all, he hadn't needed high-tech labs and state-of-the-art equipment to prove he was a great robot designer.

As they walked down a narrow lane between two rickety towers, their footsteps echoed in the silence of the evening. George switched on his flashlight. At the end of the lane was a mountain of scrap iron. George spotted a rusting wheelbarrow and pulled it free. The heap of iron tipped dangerously, then settled again. "This'll come in handy if we find something worth taking," George said.

"But what are we looking for?" Anne asked.

"Anything that looks useful," George said.

He began to dig around in the pile, and Anne followed suit. "How about this?" she asked, pulling out a metal tool.

"Nice! An adjustable wrench," George said. "Put it in the wheelbarrow."

"Woof!" said Sparky. "Woof, woof, woof!" His head went up and down and his iron tail wagged.

"Hey, look, his Fetch program's been activated! He thinks this is a game," Anne said. "Go on, Sparky —fetch!"

She drew back her arm and hurled the wrench. Sparky scampered after it. The wrench bounced and clanked along the ground before disappearing under a stack of cars. The robot dog squirmed in after it. George heard a scrabbling sound from beneath the pile of cars. Then Sparky started to whimper.

"Oh, no," Anne moaned. "He's stuck!" They ran to the car stack. George pulled away a dirty tarp that was hanging on the bottom of the pile and shined a flashlight beneath. Sparky was whining with panic. "Sparky!" Anne called. "Lie down flat!"

The robot dog obeyed. George and Anne got down on their bellies and, reaching into the darkness, grabbed a paw each and pulled Sparky to safety. He still had the adjustable wrench in his mouth, and looked as if he was grinning.

"You silly dog!" Anne said.

George got up and dusted himself off. Suddenly he stopped moving and stared at the bottom car, no longer obscured by the tarp.

No. It couldn't be.

He turned the flashlight on it and gasped. It was. He took a step closer, a chill crawling over his body.

"George? What's wrong?" Anne asked. "You look like you've seen a ghost!"

"That . . . car," George said slowly. "The Wheeltech Prodigy. It was my parents' car. I'm sure of it."

"But—but there must be hundreds of old Prodigys," Anne stammered. "They were one of the first smartcars on the market, weren't they? How can you be sure it's theirs?"

"I recognize it," George said. "I have an old photo of it in my scrapbook, loaded up for a camping trip to Phish Lake. It was pale blue, just like this. And look!" He shone the flashlight on the back of the car—and there was a faded sticker that read I LEFT MY HEART AT PHISH LAKE.

"Wow," Anne said. She looked like she was full of questions, but didn't say anything more. George knew she was curious. He'd never told her how they had died.

"It's okay, I don't mind talking about it," George said. "My parents died in a car accident—they were driving out of Terabyte Heights and lost control of the car. It swerved off the side of the road and fell into the river. There's a safety barrier there now, I think." George touched the scratched surface of the car door and swallowed the lump in his throat. "I never would have seen this if I hadn't pulled that tarp off to find Sparky. I had no idea Otto even had the car — he never told me it was here."

"Well, why would he?" said Anne. "He probably figured you didn't want to be reminded about what happened."

"Maybe not before," George muttered. "But now I need to know the truth."

Sparky was snuffling around under the Prodigy and barked again. "What is it, boy?" Anne said.

George shone his flashlight beneath the car, and saw something shiny reflect the light back toward him. He got down on his hands and knees for a closer look.

"Well?" asked Anne.

George wasn't sure what he was looking at. "It looks like a cover, some sort of hatch on top of the ground!"

He was trying to squeeze closer when he felt a vibra-

tion coming from his pocket. Still on his belly, he pulled out his marble. It was glowing bright blue and reverberating with a low hum. It looked strange and magical in the darkness, like a miniature planet in his palm.

Anne's eyes widened. "What's that?"

"Something my dad gave me before he died," George said, and explained about the strange message that appeared when he was first inside TinkerTech.

Anne stared at the glowing marble with wonder. "So you think Project Mercury might be something your parents worked on?" she said.

"I can't be sure," George admitted. "But I think Micron might know."

Anne's jaw clenched at the mention of his name.

"The marble lit up red today when I was outside his old office," George continued.

He struggled to edge closer. "We need to get to that hatch. Can you shine the flashlight while I hold the marble near it?"

They both lay down flat and George crawled on his elbows toward the hatch. The marble's color intensified. He banged his head on the underside of the car. "Ouch!"

Anne aimed the flashlight. "What do you see?"

"There's *something* on the hatch," George said. He squeezed himself as close as he could get. "There's a weird symbol in the middle."

"What does it look like?"

"Like a circle with horns, with a tail like an upside-down cross."

George backed out again. With the tip of his shoe, he drew the symbol on the dusty ground. "Any idea what it means?"

Anne shook her head. "Looks like some kind of ancient sign."

"Whatever it is, it's important. I'm sure of it!" George said. "If I could open that hatch, who knows what I'd find inside?"

"Well, you can't," Anne

said. "Because there's a great big pile of cars on top of it. Unless . . ."

She was staring up at the tall dark shape of the crane and its magnet, silhouetted against the purple evening sky.

George followed her gaze. "No way!" he said. "We can't do that!"

"Can't we?" she said, with a mischievous grin. "Do you want to get into that hatch or not?"

"But I don't know how to operate it," said George. "My uncle's never let me near the thing."

Anne shrugged. "Well, he isn't here now, is he?"

George admired Anne's nerve. And he had secretly always wanted to operate the magnetic crane. Besides, it was the only way he was going to find out what was hidden beneath his parents' car . . .

"All right," he said. "Let's—"

CLANG! CLANG!

"What's that?" said Anne, spinning around.

George felt a knot in the pit of his stomach. There shouldn't be anyone else here.

CLANG! CLANG!

Sparky growled, low and deep.

CLANG! CLANG!

At the far end of the lane between the two stacks of cars, George saw an impossibly tall figure striding toward them. Its huge feet shook the ground with every step. From what George could make out in the semidarkness, it had a pointed head and sinister, shining black eyes.

"Trespassers detected!" it said.

George looked at Anne, and saw the terror he felt reflected in her face.

"Where did that thing come from?" whispered Anne.

"I don't know," George said. "But it doesn't look friendly."

"No kidding, genius!"

"Trespassers will be neutralized!" the robot said. It pointed both arms at them, and George saw that each arm ended in a thin metal tube, like the barrel of a gun.

"Get down!" shouted George. He grabbed Anne by the wrist and they threw themselves flat on the ground. A second later, two streaks of lightning shot from the

robot's hands and struck the stack of cars behind them with a blast of sound. George turned to see two sizzling, smoking patches of metal where the lightning had made contact.

"It's trying to kill us!" Anne shouted.

"Trespassers will be neutralized!" repeated the robot.

"We're not trespassers!" George shouted. "This is my uncle's junkyard!"

"Negative. This junkyard is now the property of Mr. Freezie. Trespassers will be neutralized!"

CLANG! CLANG! CLANG! CLANG!

It rushed toward them, its weapons aimed squarely at their heads.

"Quick! Move!" said George. They both rolled to one side as the electric bolts hit the spot they'd just occupied. Sparky ran in a circle, farting wildly.

"This way!" Anne said. She jumped to her feet and, pulling George by the arm, dodged around the edge of the stack of cars. For the moment, they had a wall of rusting iron between them and the robot.

CLANG! CLANG!

"Whoever Mr. Freezie, is, he doesn't like guests, does he?" said Anne.

The ominous sound of robotic footsteps came closer. George saw Sparky standing his ground at the end of the path between the stacks of cars, barking defiantly. Suddenly there was a flash, and Sparky was engulfed in a crackling blue haze. His ears and tail stood on end, fizzing with sparks.

"That bucket of bolts got Sparky!" Anne screamed.

The blue haze disappeared. "Woof!" said Sparky, then scampered to Anne's side.

"Whew," said Anne, and hugged him with relief. "It takes more than that to keep you down, doesn't it, boy?"

George hated to think of the damage one of those blasts would do to him or Anne though. They certainly wouldn't be up and running with their tails wagging.

CLANG! CLANG!

George, Anne, and Sparky ducked behind an old refrigerator just as the security-bot rounded the corner. It stopped, and scanned the area.

An idea popped into George's desperate brain.

"Can you make Sparky run over there?" he whispered to Anne, pointing. "Just under the magnetic crane?"

Anne grinned—George could see she'd gotten the idea. "Good thinking, Robot Boy," she said.

"Heat source detected!" the security-bot announced. *"Trespassers will be neutralized!"*

It lumbered toward their hiding place.

Anne grabbed a wrench and showed it to Sparky. "Fetch, boy!" She hurled the tool and it landed right beneath the crane. Sparky bounded after it.

"Trespassers will be neutralized!" the robot repeated.

"Taser fire ineffective. Crushing method initiated."

It started stamping toward the robot dog.

"Run, Sparky!" Anne shouted. "Run fast!"

"I'm on it!" George said.

He squeezed behind the fridge and came out in the path behind it, parallel to the one with the security-bot. He sprinted toward the crane, leaping over piles of scrap as he went.

CLANG! CLANG!

"Woof! Woof!"

George reached the crane, clambered up to the door, and threw himself into the driver's seat. Through the windshield, he saw Sparky with the wrench in his mouth as the security-bot approached.

Sparky whined, and sank to the ground on his belly.

George quickly scanned the dashboard. A big red button was labeled START. *Easy enough,* George thought. He pushed it, and the engine roared to life.

The security-bot stopped and looked straight at George. Its eyes flashed blue, and it prepared to fire.

On the dash, George saw another button marked ACTIVATE MAGNET.

George smiled. "Hey, big guy!" he called to the security-bot. The hulking machine cocked its head, listening. "Neutralize this!" George shouted, and hit the button.

Instantly, the security-bot flew up into the air, and its head struck the underside of the magnet with a noise like the banging of a colossal gong. The impact crumpled its pointy head, and in the next moment there was another flurry of gong strikes as its arms and legs all hit the magnet and stuck fast.

Anne ran out to Sparky. George slid down from the cab and joined her.

"Nice one!" Anne said, reaching out for a fist bump. "So what do we do about him?" she added, nodding up at the dangling robot.

"Let him hang out with the rest of the junk," said George. "C'mon, let's get out of here."

5

An hour later, they arrived back at George's house. Their clothes were torn and filthy, and they smelled of exhaust and engine oil. The only one who seemed to be in good spirits was Sparky. He still had the wrench clamped in his mouth, and his tail was wagging furiously.

"I'm going home," Anne said, rubbing her eyes. "If my dad finds out I'm gone at this hour, I'm toast."

"Yeah . . ." mumbled George, distracted. He couldn't stop thinking about the mysterious symbol in the junkyard. What did it have to do with his parents?

"Look, we'll figure out what's beneath that hatch door, don't worry," Anne said, as if reading his thoughts.

Then, within a few seconds, she and Sparky had vanished into the night.

When George walked in the door, Otto was staring at his tablet, searching through a digital menswear catalog and sipping coffee from a chipped mug.

"What do you think of these threads, huh, George?" he asked. He pointed to a black silk shirt embroidered all over with tiny red screwdrivers. "Pretty sharp, huh? I could wear it to the barbecue! Wouldn't that look good with my new gold necklace?"

"The only place that shirt would look good is in a fireplace," George said. "Listen, Otto. Who bought the junkyard, exactly? And why does he want it?"

"Oh, some guy named Freezie," Otto said absently, as he continued to scroll through the catalog. "Apparently he wants to turn it into an ice cream factory, so that should appeal to you. Hey, what do you think of these green leather pants?"

"For a guy who just wants to sell ice cream, he seems

to be really worried about break-ins," George said. "He's already got a huge security-bot guarding the junkyard!"

"Well, it's his business now how he owns the place," Otto said, shrugging. "We already signed all the papers. He gave me a deposit check and said he would wire me the rest by the end of the week. Once I get all the money, I'm planning on totally changing my wardrobe! Do you think I'd look good in a top hat?"

George rolled his eyes. "Hey, I found something unexpected at the junkyard," George said. He took a deep breath and said, "Mom and Dad's old car."

Otto slowly placed the tablet on the table. "Oh, that," he murmured. "To be honest, I'd forgotten it was even there. The police released it to me after they fished it out of the river. It was totaled, of course. Some things just can't be fixed, George." Otto looked at his nephew, his eyes full of grief. George was reminded that he wasn't the only one who had lost family that day.

A few seconds later, Otto cleared his throat and looked down at his big hands, which wrapped tightly around the coffee mug. "Anyway, after that I just put it in the yard and tried to forget about it. Guess I succeeded." He took a long gulp of coffee.

"But there's something underneath it," George pressed. "Like, some kind of door in the ground. Do you know anything about that?"

"Door?" Otto spluttered, almost choking on the coffee. "There's no door there. That's . . . that's ridiculous. You must've seen a panel or something, a piece of scrap. Definitely not a door." He abruptly rose from his chair. "Well, it's been quite a day. Guess I'll take a shower and go to bed. There's leftovers in the fridge if you want them." And before George could say another word, Otto was clomping up the stairs.

"Otto!" George called out after his uncle, but the bathroom door clicked shut.

He's hiding something, thought George.

After making himself a grilled cheese sandwich, George went up to his room to see how Jackbot was doing. He found his best friend sitting at the desk surrounded by crumpled-up pieces of paper, his head in his hands.

"Well! You've been . . . busy," George said.

"It's hopeless!" Jackbot said miserably. "I've analyzed all of Shakespeare's sonnets, as well as the complete works of Sappho, Catullus, Petrarch, and John Donne. The greatest love poets of all time! But no matter how hard I try to synthesize their writing techniques into my programming, I just can't do what they do. I've tried and tried, but it's not working."

"Oh, come on now," George said. "It can't be all that bad. Read me a little bit—you're probably being too hard on yourself."

"Well, if you think so," said Jackbot, reluctantly. He smoothed out one of the crumpled pieces of paper, struck a theatrical pose, and recited: "'Take my love, O Cookie, take it all; Take my cogs, my gears, my proximity sensors. But if you don't mind, leave my central processor, because without it I will no longer perform optimally.' Hmm . . . you know, maybe it isn't that bad!"

"Not for a first draft," said George, attempting an encouraging smile.

Jackbot's head slumped again, and he let the paper fall

from his hand. "I don't know what to do," he groaned. "If my poetry's no good, how will she know how I feel?"

"Why don't you try taking your mind off Cookie for a while?" George suggested. "I need your help. Can you tell me what this means?"

He picked up the sheet of paper Jackbot had dropped, and on the back he drew the symbol that had appeared on the hatch.

"Sure," Jackbot said at once. "That's the old alchemical symbol for mercury."

The hairs on the back of George's neck stood on end. *As in Project Mercury . . .*

He was on to something. And homicidal security-bots or no, he had to go back to the junkyard to find out exactly what it was.

"Thanks, Jackbot," George said. "That's a big help."

"Not for *me*," Jackbot said. "It only took my mind off Cookie for eight-tenths of a second."

"Otto, please," George shouted. "I'm begging you— make it stop!"

"Oh, quit your bellyaching," Otto yelled back. "It's only opera."

The truck's stereo was blaring as Otto drove George and Jackbot to TinkerTech the next morning. A woman was singing in Italian over a blast of orchestral music, her voice soaring up and down like she was on some kind of nightmarish roller coaster.

"It's Verdi's *Aida*," Jackbot said. "*Another* tale of unrequited love."

"I don't get it. You hate opera," George said, unplugging his fingers from his ears as the song ended.

"Not anymore," Otto said. "I've moved up in the world, so naturally I listen to high-class stuff."

As the next song began, Otto turned the stereo up

even louder. George felt like the noise was piercing his skull.

"We could jump out here," he said, as the truck approached a traffic jam and slowed down. "It's only a couple of blocks up the road."

"You want to take the old ankle express, that's fine by me!" Otto said.

George and Jackbot climbed out and made their way along the sidewalk toward TinkerTech HQ.

"Today is going to be different, Jackbot," George said. "I won't let Patricia get on my nerves, and I'll be such a model apprentice that they'll have to put me back on robotics! And I'm going to figure out a way to get into Micron's office."

"I aim to have a better day too," Jackbot said. "I have a foolproof plan to win Cookie's heart!"

"So you were able to finish a love poem?" asked George.

"No," said Jackbot. "I stayed up all night watching soap operas on TV. Shakespeare didn't have a clue!

Those shows gave me a much better idea than some stuffy poem."

Uh-oh, George thought.

As they approached TinkerTech, George decided it would be quicker to cut across the parking lot.

He had only taken two steps off the curb into the lot when Jackbot shoved him to the ground. "Hey!" George cried as he hit the asphalt. A second later a red sports car whizzed by, so close that the wind it created ruffled George's hair. Half a block ahead, the car screeched to a halt.

"Phew!" George panted, getting to his feet. "That car could have killed me. Thanks, Jackbot."

"Think nothing of it," Jackbot said. "I would have had a harder time putting you back together than you had with me!"

A young woman jumped out of the car. She had a TinkerTech nametag on the lapel of her navy-blue business suit. "I'm so sorry!" she said, wringing her hands in worry. "Are you all right? I don't know what happened

—I was listening to the news on my MOD and my mind must have wandered."

George saw that she was wearing the small white earpiece, and her eyes were shiny, illuminated by the nanocircuitry in her contact lenses. "How do you already have a MOD?" he asked, surprised. "They haven't been released yet."

"I'm a beta tester," the woman explained. "I was told to use it all the time—never take it off. I'm supposed to evaluate its safety features."

"They don't seem to be working," George said.

"I'll—I'll be sure to mention it," she said, looking down, embarrassed. Then she got back in her car and quickly drove off.

• • •

"Good morning, George Gearing," said the security-bot as George and Jackbot entered the building. "Good morning, Doctor Jack." George rolled his eyes.

They took the elevator to the fifteenth floor, where Mr. Volt, Patricia, and Cookie were already waiting.

"Hi, George!" Patricia said in a singsong voice. "Ready for cleaning duty? Scrub, scrub, scrubbety-dub!"

George didn't take the bait. Instead he turned to Mr. Volt. "Is Professor Droid around, sir? I really need to speak with him."

"Hello, Cookie," Jackbot said. He walked up to the hovering robot, who was buffing Patricia's nails with a spinning arm attachment. "Darling, we need to talk."

The buffer kept spinning. "Commence communication," Cookie said coldly.

"There's something special between us," Jackbot said dramatically. "You know it. I know it. But we can't act on those feelings, Cookie! We just can't! Because . . . there's someone else."

The buffer went still. "Explain." Cookie said.

"Yes," Jackbot said seriously. "Her name is Olympia;

she's a four-door sedan. And she's madly in love with me."

Cookie took out a bottle of polish and began painting Patricia's nails.

"But it's really important!" George was saying to Patricia's father. "It's about the MOD."

"If you have any concerns, you can tell me," said Volt. "I'll pass them on to Professor Droid."

"I nearly got run over in the parking lot," George said, "by a woman who was wearing the MOD! It's dangerous, and it needs to be fixed before everyone starts wearing them!"

"That issue has already been addressed," Volt answered. "Because we don't completely understand the sophisticated device, our safety testing has been comprehensive. But the MOD shuts off when the wearer is driving—I'm sure of it."

"The woman *was* driving! And the MOD didn't shut off! How do you explain that?" George said. "If you would just let me *analyze* one, I know I could—"

"Look, George," Volt said. He put his hand on

George's shoulder, a mask of insincerity on his face. "You've been through a lot in these past few months. After almost losing your life and being hunted by a criminal mastermind, it's natural to see danger lurking everywhere. It's understandable that you would be afraid. But there is *no* danger anymore."

Meanwhile, Jackbot was standing at the window, facing away from Cookie and massaging his temples. "If I break Olympia's heart—there's no telling what she might do. So you see—you and I can never be together!" He sneaked a look at Cookie. "Doesn't that make you want me all the more?"

Cookie's LED eyes flashed. "No," she said.

"But I'm *not* afraid!" George was protesting. "Did the security-bot tell you that? Jackbot just made up that stuff about me having PTSD so he could get into the building!"

Volt shook his head. "Acceptance is the first step toward healing, George."

There was a humming sound, and the huge form of the OCD-bot came gliding around the corner. It was holding a squeegee mop and had a bucket balanced on its head.

"Cleaning things is my delight!" it sang. "Today we'll make the windows bright!"

George's heart sank. TinkerTech was almost entirely made of glass. "How many windows *are* there?" he asked.

The robot twirled the mop. "Let me see, now, let me see—seven hundred ninety-three!"

George groaned.

"Off you go," Patricia said. "Those windows won't wash themselves!"

6

He had only been at TinkerTech for an hour, and already George's day needed a reboot. He was not going to waste another minute washing windows when he could be building robots. But since it wasn't likely they were going to let him anywhere near a robotics workshop, he figured he would do the next best thing.

Break into Micron's old office.

He just needed to ditch the OCD-bot somehow. George wracked his brain trying to come up with a plan of escape as he and Jackbot followed the robot down the hallway toward the elevators.

Jackbot was moping. "I don't understand why that didn't work," he complained. "In all the soap operas I

watched, jealousy made the guy impossible to resist!" He sighed.

Just then, George noticed a bank of vending machines opposite the elevator, and a plan jumped fully formed into his mind.

"Excuse me, OCD-bot?" George said. "Do you mind if I stop and get a hot chocolate?"

"If you must, then yes, you may," the OCD-bot said, a trifle grumpily. "Be quick! We have a busy day!"

"Jackbot," George muttered under his breath. "Call the elevator."

The elevator doors opened just as George's hot chocolate finished pouring. George took the Styrofoam cup and walked toward the doors. But as he reached them, he pretended to trip, and sloshed the entire contents of the cup onto the elevator floor.

"Now you've made a dreadful mess!" complained the OCD-bot. "Dreadful messes cause distress!"

The robot rolled into the elevator and started swabbing the floor. George pressed the button for the fiftieth floor and darted out of the elevator right as the doors closed, with the OCD-bot still inside.

"That should keep him busy for a while," George said.

"How clever, sly, and ingenious of you," Jackbot said, nodding appreciatively. "Where are we going now?"

"Micron's office, where else? C'mon, before anybody sees us!"

Micron's unoccupied office was still covered with police tape. George pulled the marble from his pocket and saw that it was glowing a deep crimson, just like before.

George shot a quick look up and down the corridor. Without a word, he and Jackbot climbed over the police tape, entered the office, and eased the door shut behind them.

The stainless steel walls were blank and there was no furniture, not even a computer. The room was completely bare. It was like being inside a large metal cube. George felt his hope dissolve into disappointment.

"Identify yourself!" said an electronic voice from a

speaker on the ceiling. George jumped. "Password, please!" it demanded.

"Um . . ." said George.

"Master of the Universe!" said Jackbot.

"Jackbot!" George muttered. "What are you doing? We're going to get caught!"

But instead of sounding the alarm, the voice said, "Good morning, Chip!"

An elegant chrome and leather chair suddenly rose from the floor, along with a glass and metal desk with a sleek computer monitor attached. Pictures flipped out of the walls all over the room, mostly of Micron smiling and looking pleased with himself, and holding his many awards he'd won. But some were also group photos that looked like graduation pictures. A slender, brushed-steel robot emerged from a cupboard, placed a steaming cup of tea on the desk, then disappeared back into the cabinet.

"Impressive," Jackbot said.

"I don't get it," George said. "How did you know the password?"

Jackbot tapped the side of his head. "When Micron kidnapped me, he let me see all kinds of private information. I guess he figured I wouldn't be around long enough to use it."

"Well, he sure was wrong about that!" George said, grinning. He slid into Micron's chair and cracked his knuckles. "Now, let's get hacking, shall we?" George looked at the empty desk and frowned. "Where's the keyboard and stuff?" He put his hands on the glass surface, and the moment his fingers made contact, a digital keyboard lit up right beneath them. "Nice," he said.

George booted up the machine and clicked through Micron's files until he found a list of folders. "Annual report," he muttered, scrolling down. "Research and development, MOD strategy . . ." And then his breath caught in his throat.

There it was: a folder called "Project Mercury."

"This is it, Jackbot!" he said. "We found it!"

He clicked on the folder. Immediately a dialog box popped up: ENTER PASSWORD.

"Yeah, yeah," George said, and typed in MASTER OF THE UNIVERSE before pressing OK.

But the folder did not open. Instead, an angry-looking red dialogue box appeared around the words: INCORRECT PASSWORD! ACCESS DENIED!

George's sighed. "Did he mention another password, by any chance?"

"No," Jackbot answered. "Sorry, buddy."

"Well, I'll just have to guess." George thought hard. *Micron is an egomaniac . . . maybe he'd use his own name.* He typed in MICRON.

The red box began to flash. INCORRECT PASSWORD, it read. ACCESS DENIED. ONE MORE INCORRECT ATTEMPT WILL RESULT IN DELETION OF THE FILE.

George pushed away from the keyboard, dejected. "I can't risk being wrong again," he said. "If this file gets erased, I'll never find out the truth about my parents."

Jackbot looked thoughtful. "If I download the folder onto my hard drive, we can work on cracking it at home."

"That's perfect!" George said, a spark of hope rising in him again. "Do it!"

Jackbot pulled a cable from his chest cavity and inserted the plug into one of the monitor's USB ports. A bar appeared on the screen, counting off the megabytes. It moved agonizingly slow. *A big file . . .*

When it was halfway done, a voice piped up from outside the door. "I'm searching for my trusty team!" it sang. "We're going to make this building gleam!"

"The OCD-bot!" George whispered in alarm. The door began to open. "Jackbot, get down!"

They both dived behind the desk. Jackbot's cable was still plugged into the port—George hoped it couldn't be seen from the doorway.

George heard the OCD-bot roll into the room, then stop. In the silence, George could hear his heart hammering in his ears. If it caught them now, Jackbot couldn't finish the download—and they might never get a second chance. His apprenticeship would be over, and they'd probably never let George get within a mile of TinkerTech again.

As he crouched there, willing the robot to leave, George realized he was staring at a photograph on the wall to the side of the desk. It showed two men with a group of teenagers, most likely college students by the look of them. George studied the men's faces; why did they look so familiar? Then he saw them—it was

Micron and Professor Droid! They had to be at least ten years younger. What were they doing with all those students? George squinted to read the photo's caption: BRIGHT MINDS PROGRAM: CLASS OF . . . He tried to make out the number, but he was too far away to read it.

George heard the office door close with a sharp click. The OCD-bot had left the room! He let out a long sigh of relief.

"Download complete!" Jackbot announced.

"Thank goodness," George said. He stood up and peered more closely at the photo. There was something about the faces of two of the college kids, a boy and a girl, standing right next to Micron. They looked so familiar . . .

And then it dawned on him.

George had only seen more recent photos, but he knew their faces, deep in his heart. His mother's short black hair and crooked grin. His father's wiry frame and the sparkle in his eyes as he stood with an arm casually thrown around George's mother's shoulders. It must have been only a few years before they got married—before George was born. Before . . .

George's eyes stung. He had to look away.

"Jackbot," he said softly. "Come look at this."

"That's how Dr. Micron knew them," Jackbot said. "One more piece of the puzzle."

"GEORGE GEARING, PLEASE REPORT TO DEPARTMENT SIX IMMEDIATELY! THE OCD-BOT IS LOOKING FOR YOU!" Mr. Volt's voice burst out over the PA system.

"We'd better go," George said. "Anyway, we got what we came for."

Jackbot nodded and made his way out of the office. George was about to follow, but hesitated. He took one last look at the smiling faces of his parents, frozen forever in that happy moment. "I won't let you down," George whispered, and ran out the door.

"Just follow the path; the party is in the yard,"
said the butler-bot on the front lawn of Professor Droid's
house.

"Yard" wasn't really an adequate description. Droid's
lawn was the size of two football fields. George, Otto,
and Jackbot passed the tennis courts, crossed an
orchard, and joined the other guests on a wide, elevated
terrace that was adorned with statues of obsolete robots.
A robot in a red and white checkered apron was flip-
ping burgers and steaks on a charcoal grill, filling the
air with smells that made George's mouth water. On a
lower terrace, a quartet of automated string instruments
were playing themselves.

"This place sure is something," said Otto.

"A bit like your outfit," said Jackbot.

George winced as he looked again at his uncle. True to his word, Otto had accompanied George to the party, eager to start his new life as a member of Terabyte Heights' elite. He had spent several hours at the store the day before, selecting new clothes to impress at the barbecue, and George wondered if the sales assistant had played some sort of trick on him. He was wearing a mustard yellow polyester suit, complete with lime green loafers, a red silk tie, and a pink carnation in his lapel. He looked like something out of a coloring book. Any one of these items was strange in itself, but the combination made George feel nauseated.

"Canapé, sir?" said a waiter-bot, holding out a tray of delicacies.

"Don't mind if I do!" said Otto, taking the whole tray and popping two hors d'oeuvres into his mouth. "Got anything to drink?"

The waiter-bot was silent, clearly trying to process his lack of manners.

"It's okay, buddy," said Otto. "I can see a drink-bot

over there." He tossed another pastry into his mouth and pointed at George. "Stay out of trouble, okay?" Then, like a clown on the loose from a circus, he strode off toward a robot that was holding a tray of punch glasses.

George spotted Anne standing beneath a cherry tree, its branches bright with blossoms under the midday sun. He waved to her and she smiled. "Come on, Jackbot," said George.

Jackbot was craning his neck left and right, and didn't seem to hear him.

"Hey, JB," said George. "What's up?"

"I'm looking for Cookie," said Jackbot. "Do you see her?"

George looked around and shook his head. "I'm sure Patricia Volt will be around, though," he said.

"I hope so," said Jackbot. "I've written two sonnets, but one relies on good weather for full effect. The other employs a complex metrical scheme which may be compromised by the music from those robotic instruments."

"Relax," said George. "You're just nervous."

"Hey, George," said Anne, as they approached. "Glad you could make it."

"Your dad certainly knows how to throw a party!"

"This is nothing," Anne said. "You should see the place at Christmas—it's like the North Pole meets Times Square." She squinted back at the house. "I wonder where he is. It's not like him to be late for his own party."

"I'm sure he'll make an appearance soon," George said. "Thanks again for inviting us."

"Your uncle seems to be having a good time," Anne observed with a grin. She nodded toward the terrace, where Otto had balanced the empty canapé tray on top of a statue. There were crumbs all over his shirt, and he had a drink in each hand. The other guests were keeping their distance.

"He's not my uncle!" George said. "I've never met him before in my life."

Anne laughed. "He's enjoying himself, that's all."

"In other news," George said to Anne, "you know that weird symbol we found at the junkyard? Jackbot told me what it means. Tell her, JB."

But Jackbot was jogging across the terrace toward the Volts, where George saw Cookie hovering in the air next to Patricia.

"Oh no, he's going to make a fool of himself again!" said George.

"So what's this about the symbol?" Anne asked.

George tore his attention away from Jackbot. Anne's eyes were bright and curious.

"You were right—it *is* an ancient symbol," George said. "For mercury! It has to be linked with Project Mercury, don't you think? And I found a file with that name on Micron's computer—"

"Whoa! You hacked into Micron's computer?" Anne was suddenly serious.

George blinked. It was easy to forget that while Anne was his best friend, she was also Professor Droid's daughter. "Yeah . . ."

"Look, I appreciate a good computer hack as much as the next girl," Anne whispered. "But I know how tight the TinkerTech mainframe is, and that sort of thing can be traced. If my dad found out you were digging up top secret information, that apprenticeship of yours would be nothing more than a distant memory. He's a stickler for rules, George—believe me, I know!"

"But my parents were working on something top secret," said George, "and it may have gotten them killed."

"Wait, what do you mean, 'killed'? I thought they died in a car crash."

"Yes, but you know what Micron said. He told me they crossed him and paid for it."

Anne studied George's face. "You're really serious about this, aren't you?" she asked.

"As serious as I've ever been in my life," George replied.

Anne sighed. "I was afraid of that. Well, whatever you've got in mind, it isn't going to be easy."

George grinned. "Is it ever?" He was about to go into more detail about what he had found in Micron's office when he was cut off by the sound of applause.

Professor Droid emerged through the French doors onto the terrace, and the music died. He was dressed in an immaculate, cream-colored suit, and George could see the white bud of the MOD peeking out from his ear. The lenses made his eyes shine in that strange way that meant the device was connected to his brain. George imagined that Droid probably had the text of his speech streaming right in front of him. Yet another amazing thing that the MOD could do.

"Thanks for coming, everyone!" Professor Droid said. "I'd like to say a few words if I may."

Despite his expensive suit and the high-tech addition, George thought Anne's father looked tired. There were bags under his eyes, and his jaw was covered with a hard shadow of stubble. Anne had told him her father sometimes didn't come back from the office at night, preferring to catch a little sleep there and be onsite to troubleshoot any last minute problems.

"Thank you very much for joining me on the eve of such a *momentous* occasion," Professor Droid said. "As you all know, we're here to celebrate the launch of the MOD, which, come tomorrow, will officially be released to the public." Polite applause followed. "This ingenious device will *revolutionize* our way of life," Droid continued, "more than any single piece of technology in history, aside from the wheel, of course." A murmur of laughter passed through the crowd. "You know, our critics say a dependence on technology makes us less human, by taking away personal interaction and replacing it with screens and processors. But I think the opposite is true. The MOD enterprise will connect the entire world. We'll be able to talk to one another in new ways, sharing knowledge more creatively than ever before. It is thanks to the great minds of TinkerTech — some of whom are among us today — that this launch was made possible. Because of them, lives everywhere will be forever changed." He raised his arms above his head, in a gesture meant to encompass everything around him. "Tomorrow, Terabyte Heights—after that, the world!"

George clapped halfheartedly, and saw that Anne wasn't clapping with much enthusiasm either. Although Droid's words were obviously meant to be inspiring, there was something flat about the way he'd said them. Robotic, even.

"Now, are there any questions?" Droid asked.

An African American woman with horn-rimmed glasses put her hand up. "Hello, Professor—I'm Wanda Vector from the *Terabyte Tablet*. I just wanted to ask about Charles Micron. He still hasn't been located by the police. How can you be sure he won't return to try to sabotage this project?"

George saw Droid's face twitch slightly, as if the reporter had struck a nerve. But Droid recovered quickly. "That's a very good question, Ms. Vector," he said smoothly. "But you have nothing to worry about.

Dr. Micron no longer has any access to TinkerTech systems, and all of his accounts have been frozen. If he so much as sets foot in Terabyte Heights, he'll be arrested on the spot. I promise you, he is no longer a threat to this town. Set your minds at ease, ladies and gentlemen—and enjoy the party!"

The crowd dispersed to pile their plates with barbecue. George shot a sidelong glance at Anne. "Your dad sounded a little . . . weird, don't you think?" he said to her. "And how can he be so sure that Micron's out of the picture?"

Anne bit her lip. "He *did* sound a little off, but he's been really stressed out lately, so that probably explains it. And as far as Micron is concerned—"

In the next moment, one of the gardener-bots appeared at George's side. It was a stout little steel robot, painted green and covered in dirt. It had a sprinkler on top of its head that looked like a beanie cap, and a roll of water hose curled at its side like a cowboy's lasso.

"Excuse me, sir? Sorry to interrupt, but do you own a robot by the name of Jackbot?"

"Yes. Why? What's he doing?"

"Destroying the garden, sir."

"What? Jackbot wouldn't do that!" George said.

"If you would care to follow me . . ."

George sighed. "Okay. Anne, I'll be back in a sec."

He followed the gardener-bot. They passed Otto, who was loudly telling another guest about how he wouldn't miss the junkyard one bit. George looked in the other direction before Otto could catch his eye, and as he did something flashed in the branches of a tree. George stopped dead. Whatever it was, it was glinting among the leaves, and panic seized his chest. He was almost sure it was one of Micron's moth-bots—little winged assassins that squirted deadly acid on their victims. George had been attacked by one before and wasn't likely to forget it. But as he pressed closer, a breeze stirred the leaves and the flash was gone.

I'm being paranoid, he told himself. The conversation with Anne had made him feel jumpy, that was all.

George hurried to catch up with the gardener-bot. "This way," it urged him politely. George followed it around the side of Droid's mansion, and there in the middle of a flower bed stood Jackbot. His arms so were full of blossoms that George could barely see his face over the top of them: roses of every color. Behind him, George saw blank patches of dirt, interspersed with flattened flowers.

"Jackbot!" shouted George. "What do you think you're doing?"

"Cookie's response to my poetry was not as good as I expected, so I've moved to plan B. I'm gathering a bouquet."

"But Jackbot. You can't just—"

"Flowers speak the language of love, George," Jackbot said. "I thought everyone knew that."

He trotted past George, like a mobile flower show, toward the throng of guests.

"I'm sorry," George said to the gardener-bot. "I'll pay for the damage. At least, my uncle will."

He took off after Jackbot, catching up just as the robot reached Cookie.

"Roses are red," Jackbot recited to her. "Violets are

blue. TTL converter cables are nice, but not as nice as you!"

The Volts stared at Jackbot in disdain, and Cookie hovered above him, her blue LED eyes studying the bouquet. "Why would I wish to receive this pile of dead vegetable matter?"

"Because you're madly in love with me?" Jackbot said hopefully.

The Volts and some of the other guests burst out laughing. Patricia was busy recording the entire episode with her phone. "This is *so* going on my blog tomorrow!" she chortled.

"Of course!" said Jackbot. "You'd prefer chocolates!"

The laughter intensified.

George grabbed Jackbot's shoulder and marched him clear of the Volts. "Jackbot—give it up!" he muttered fiercely.

"What have I done wrong?" Jackbot said. "Women like thoughtful gifts. All the books say so!"

"She's not a woman," said George. "She's a robot, and she doesn't like you! Get that into your silly metal skull!"

Jackbot's head drooped. "Yes, I'm silly," he said sadly. "A silly little robot. Stupid, daft, foolish. That's me. Struck dumb by love."

George's anger vanished like a puff of smoke. Suddenly all he felt was guilt. He'd never yelled at Jackbot before —not once. "Look, Jackbot," he said softly, "I didn't mean—"

A silver shape flashed past against the blue sky. There could be no doubt this time. It was a moth-bot, and it was probably on its way to report to Micron . . . wherever he was.

"Dope, dweeb, loser," muttered Jackbot. He perked up a little. "So I shouldn't bother with the chocolates, you think?"

But George was already running across the terrace, threading between the guests. He had to warn Professor Droid. *Micron might not be here right now, but he's somewhere watching!*

Anne was standing with her father and a group of acquaintances. George crept up to his side.

"Professor Droid," he said quietly.

123

Droid moved a couple of paces away from the group and bent his head to listen. "Yes, young man—what is it?"

"Charles Micron is back!" George said. "I just saw one of his moth-bots."

Droid looked alarmed. He glanced around furtively. "Keep your voice down," he whispered. "We cannot afford another scene, especially with reporters around. You're probably imagining things."

"I know what I saw," George said. "One of those things tried to kill me less than a month ago!"

"Perhaps it was a real moth?" suggested Droid.

"Real moths aren't mechanical, sir," said George.

"Um, George," said Anne, who had come over to listen. "Maybe you can explain this to my dad after the party? You'll listen to him, right, Dad?"

"You have to *evacuate* the party!" said George. "Who knows what Micron is planning?"

"Did someone mention Micron?" said a voice. George turned and saw the journalist from the *Tablet* sidling over.

"No, of course not!" said Droid, glaring at George. "Ms. Vector, I'm sure you remember George Gearing. He's now one of our TinkerTech apprentices."

"Of course!" she said, grinning. "My stories made the front page for weeks thanks to you, George."

George wondered for a moment if he should tell her what he'd seen, but thought better of it. Droid's eyes were boring into him.

"Indeed," said Droid. "And he's also a very promising student of robotics, aren't you, George?"

"Um . . ."

While George was thinking of something to say, Otto's angry voice rose above the chatter of the other guests.

"Give it here!" he shouted. "You're overcooking them!"

George spotted his uncle standing alongside a cookbot near the grill. Otto was trying to wrangle the tongs from the bot's hand, without seeming to realize they were attached.

"Sir, please desist and move away from the cooking area," said the robot. "This is a fire hazard."

125

"Clamp it, tin can!" said Otto. "I've been cooking steaks since I was a kid, and I'm telling you, people like it rare—not like shoe leather!" He made another grab for the tongs, but the robot spun deftly out of the way. Otto tripped and landed butt first on the grill plate. The spectators gasped.

"*Yowwwww!*" he shouted.

Otto jumped three feet in the air, the seat of his mustard-colored pants black and smoking.

"Perhaps you and your uncle should excuse yourselves," said Mr. Volt, appearing at their side.

George sighed and rushed over to his uncle. Could this day get any worse? "Hey, Otto—c'mon, let's go home," said George.

"No way!" said his uncle, fanning his rear with a paper plate. "I'm just starting to have a good time!" He marched past George to a gardener-bot, grabbing an empty glass from a table on the way. "Fill her up. I'm feeling a little hot under the collar."

"Does not compute," said the robot.

"Otto," said George. "Please, can we go?"

Otto held up his hand. "Keep out of this, George. I think I'm speaking too fast for it." He waved his empty cup in front of the bot's face. "More. Drink. Iced. Tea?"

"Does not compute," repeated the robot.

Otto rolled his eyes. "I thought these things were supposed to make life easier," he said. "I guess I'll help myself."

"Otto, it's a gardening robot," said George, but his uncle was already prodding a series of buttons on the bot's chest panel. There was a click, and the sprinkler on top of the bot's head began to spin around.

George had less than half a second to dive to the ground before powerful jets of water spewed from the sprinkler, soaking Professor Droid, Mr. Volt, and Patricia from head to toe.

"Gardener-bot—switch off the sprinkler!" shouted Droid. "That's an order!"

The cascade stopped as abruptly as it had begun.

"My new dress!" shrieked Patricia. "It's ruined!"

"Initiate wet hair protocol," said Cookie. A hairdryer attachment sprouted from the robot's body and began to blow. Patricia batted it away.

George scanned the crowd and saw that all eyes were on him. Professor Droid was frowning. Anne shook her head sadly. Mr. Volt looked furious.

"I'm really sorry," said George, on behalf of his uncle. "Are there any towels?"

"In the pool house," said Droid, coldly. "Other side of the house. A butler-bot will accompany you."

George set off with the robot at his side, and it led him to the sparkling blue pool by the east wing. The pool house was almost as big as the house that George shared with Otto, and the door opened automatically at their approach. George had already made up his mind that they were going straight home afterward. What had promised to be a wonderful day had turned into a soggy disaster.

The robot handed him a huge stack of fluffy white towels, and took two armfuls itself.

As he followed the butler-bot back to the terrace, George could hardly see over the towels, but he heard the bot's steps falter. Then there was a strange fizzing sound.

George looked over his stack and saw that the robot had dropped the towels and that its shoulder was smoking a little. Then its limbs started to jerk. It was clearly malfunctioning.

"Foreign body contamination," it said, punching itself in the face. "Circuits compromised."

A section of its head melted away, and a moth-bot launched itself into the air as the robot began to spin in a circle. As George watched, it picked up speed, then drove itself straight into the swimming pool. A few sparks fired across its metal frame before it sank to the bottom.

George dropped all but one of the towels he was holding and ducked as the moth-bot shot over his head. He twisted and hurled the towel over the moth-bot, trapping it on the ground. George brought his foot down on top of it with a satisfying crunch.

Now he had proof to show Professor Droid that he was right about Micron and his robotic bugs. He leaned down to gather the pieces carefully in the towel.

A buzzing noise at his back sent a tingle up his spine. He felt the air go cold as a strange shadow spread over the ground. George turned slowly and found himself face-to-face with a massive swarm of deadly moth-bots.

There were too many to count. *There's more than enough deadly acid in just one of them to do serious damage!* George thought. He imagined Micron watching and listening through their built-in sensors. "Come and get me, you coward!" he said to the little buzzing monsters.

Sunlight glinted on their silvery wings as the wave of robotic insects swept toward George. Just before they reached him, George threw himself behind a lawn chair, narrowly dodging the streams of acid that shot from their bodies. He rolled and jumped to his feet again. The patio stones were sizzling.

George ran for his life. He tore around to the other

side of the pool house, but it was no use. The swarm was heading right for him.

There was no escape. This was the end. The last thing he was going to see in this life was Droid's Olympic-size swimming pool.

That's it!

Before he could think twice, George was dashing for the pool and filling his lungs with as much air as he could manage. He dove off the edge, disappearing underwater.

George swam to the bottom and grabbed the sunken body of the butler-bot to keep from floating back up to the surface. He wondered if the dark swarm was gathered above him, searching. He was safe, for now.

But he couldn't hold his breath forever.

The butler-bot stared at him with vacant eyes and for a moment George missed Jackbot terribly. He thought back to the last thing he'd said to his old friend and his *silly metal skull*, and wished he could take it all back. His lungs began to burn.

He tried to look up to see if the moth-bots were still above him, but it was hard to make out anything clearly through the blurred ripples and the sunlight.

And Anne—would Micron go after her too?

George couldn't hang on much longer. The fire in his lungs grew by the second, and he felt the sensation leaving his hands. He would have to take his chances with the moth-bots.

He placed his feet squarely on the pool floor and pushed up with every bit of strength he had left.

He soared upward and burst through the surface, gasping for air.

Silence.

Not a moth-bot in sight.

George looked around, trying to catch his breath, and saw all of the guests standing at the edge of the pool, staring at him. Jackbot was there too, looking anxiously at George.

"Oh, um . . . hi," George choked out.

"What is the meaning of this?" asked Professor Droid. His face was stony.

"How did you get past the moth-bots?"

"What moth-bots?" said Droid. "We came running because the pool alarm went off. Of course it was you, messing around—and you appear to have destroyed my butler-bot."

"You'd better come out of there, George," Otto said. Now he was the one who was embarrassed.

Patricia Volt smirked. *"How to Be the Perfect Party Guest,* by George Gearing. That's a book we're all waiting for!"

George scanned the sky. "But they were here!" he said desperately. "Look at all the burn marks!"

"I don't know what you're trying to prove with this act of vandalism," said Droid, "but I'm going to have to ask you, your uncle, and that robot of yours to leave."

George swam to the side of the pool, and Jackbot helped pull him out. George stood in front of Professor Droid, clothes dripping, and said: "Professor, I'm not making this up, I swear. Micron is behind this. We have to do something—"

"I *am* going to do something," Professor Droid said. "I'm terminating your apprenticeship."

George felt like he had been slapped in the face. He stood there, soaked and speechless.

"You've been a loose cannon since day one, George. I can't have you jeopardizing the MOD launch."

"Dad, no!" Anne said. She stepped out from behind her father. "You can't take this away—it means too much to him."

"Stay out of this, sweetheart," said Droid.

"Please, Dad," she insisted. "He's a genius, really he is!"

"I said—"

"And remember what he did for us," said Anne. "He saved your life, Dad. He saved the whole town." She looked over at the assembled party guests.

George held his breath. The other guests looked on, and seemed to be waiting to hear the answer too.

Droid cleared his throat. "All right," he said. "*One* more chance. But this is your final warning, George. One more misstep and you're fired."

"Don't worry, sir, I'll keep an eye on him," said Mr. Volt, standing by. "A very sharp eye indeed," he mumbled.

"Do you understand, George?" Droid asked.

George nodded. The war against Micron could wait until another day. He had to stay on at TinkerTech if he was ever going to learn the truth about his parents.

"I understand, sir," he said.

As they arrived back home, Otto was still grumbling about having to leave the party early, and so was Jackbot.

"I really think Cookie was warming up to me," said the robot. "I could see it in her eyes."

"Her eyes are light-emitting diodes," said George. "All you can see in them is a conductive filament."

"Hmph, you just don't understand," said Jackbot, crossing his arms. "You've never been in love."

George and Jackbot went inside while Otto was parking the truck.

"I don't know what to do," said George. "Micron is planning something, but no one believes me."

"I do," said Jackbot.

"You do?" said George.

"Of course," said Jackbot. "You're my best friend. I've got your back, no matter what happens."

George swallowed hard. "Thanks, JB. That means a lot."

"I'm glad you're still alive, by the way," said the robot. "That's three near misses in three days."

Otto came in too. "Yeah, you're pretty accident-prone at the moment. Maybe you should stay in your room for a while. Do something safe, like read a book. Stay away from robots."

"Excuse me!" said Jackbot.

"Well, except Jackbot, of course," said Otto. "Seriously, though—all these fancy-pants gizmos can be more trouble than they're worth."

George realized that Otto had a point. Still, he resented the suggestion that his recent troubles had been caused by his own clumsiness. The damage at Anne's house was caused by Micron's moth-bots, even if Professor Droid refused to believe it. That TinkerTech employee on the catwalk had *shoved* him into the machinery. And the woman who had nearly run him over—that was hardly his fault. It was the MOD.

Up in his bedroom with Jackbot, George took out his family scrapbook. It wasn't much—a few photos and birthday cards. There was a picture of all three of them beside the old blue Prodigy in the driveway at their house. They were smiling, with some pretty hills in the background. George's mother held a baby in her arms. Him. George wondered who had taken it—Otto, perhaps.

George turned the page. There was the newspaper report of their deaths. He knew it by heart.

"Two promising young robotics scientists, Arthur and Anthea Gearing, are missing and presumed dead after a tragic highway accident. Their car was pulled from the Cyan River yesterday, having crashed through the safety barrier on Route 13 outside of Terabyte Heights. Faulty brakes on their smartcar may have caused the accident. As the bodies were not found inside the vehicle, police believe they struggled free but were then swept away by the current. They leave behind a three-year-old son, George."

"So how come they were on Route 13?" asked Jackbot, peering over George's shoulder.

"Huh?" said George.

"Route 13 runs north out of town, right?" said Jackbot.

"I guess that's where we used to live," said George.

"No, you didn't," said Jackbot. He flipped back to the picture of the Prodigy. "See those hills in the background? According to my topographic files, they're to the south of Terabyte Heights."

"Are you sure?"

Jackbot nodded. "My files are accurate. Precise. Up-to-date."

George frowned. "I don't know where they were going then. But I'm betting Micron does. Speaking of Micron, how far have you gotten with decrypting that file from his office?"

"Oh, I haven't started yet," Jackbot said.

"What?" said George, feeling a bit annoyed. "Why not?"

Jackbot sighed. "It's been difficult," he said. "My feelings for Cookie—you know, I can hardly think of anything else."

George's hands gripped the scrapbook tightly, a hot rush of anger filling him. "You know, for a smart robot you're acting pretty dumb," he said. "Why can't you understand that Cookie doesn't like you? She's not programmed to like you! She doesn't have emotions."

"But *I* do. Hath not a robot hands, organs, dimensions, senses, affections, passions; fed with the same food, hurt with the same weapons, subject to the same diseases, healed by the same means, warmed and cooled by the same winter and summer as a human is?" Jackbot said, paraphrasing Shakespeare. "'If you prick us, do we not bleed?'"

"No, you don't!" George spluttered. "You're made of iron and zinc and chrome and tin and aluminum and silicon and plastic!"

There was a long silence. "Well," Jackbot said quietly. "I guess that's settled then." He got up and walked slowly from the room.

"Jackbot!" George called. But all he heard were the robot's footsteps clanking down the stairs.

What a day, George thought. He'd hurt his best

friend's feelings again, and even Anne thought he was overreacting. He'd let down Professor Droid, and Otto was embarrassed by *him* for a change!

As George slammed the scrapbook shut, he wondered if his parents would be as disappointed in him as he was in himself.

When the doorbell rang late that afternoon, the last person George expected to see standing on the porch was Mr. Volt. He had changed out of his party clothes and was dressed casually in jeans and a sweater. George noticed he was wearing a MOD earpiece and his eyes gleamed with the lens implants. He gave George a wide, white-toothed grin.

"So! Did you enjoy the barbecue this afternoon?"

"Yeah, it was a blast," George said through his teeth.

"Well, fun and games are over for now," said Volt. "The professor was kind enough to keep you on as an apprentice, so it's time to get back to work!"

"You can hardly call me an apprentice," said George.

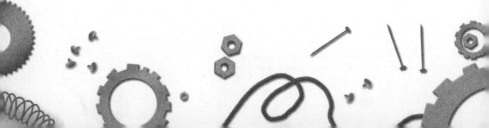

"So far the most complex technical problem I've solved is unclogging a toilet."

"Well, that could all change," said Volt. "*If* you play your cards right. We need all hands on deck at HQ tonight. Tomorrow is launch day, and we have to get every MOD device packaged up and ready to go. What do you think?"

"What—you mean now?" said George.

"You have something better to do?" said Volt.

George looked back into the living room. Otto was fast asleep and snoring. *Well, why not?* thought George. He had promised Droid he'd be a model apprentice. And maybe he'd be able to snoop around a bit at TinkerTech while he was there. "Okay, I guess. Could you please hold on a minute?"

George stepped back inside the house and walked into the kitchen. Jackbot had been sitting in there since their argument, staring out the window. He didn't even look at George.

"Jackbot, how many times can I apologize? I didn't mean what I said."

Jackbot was silent.

"I have to go to TinkerTech—will you tell Otto when he wakes up?"

"Sure," Jackbot said. "Even a stupid robot like me can manage that."

George sighed. "We'll talk more later, okay?"

"Any day now, Gearing!" Mr. Volt called from the doorway.

George hurried back outside and got into the back of Mr. Volt's expensive black car, which was driven by a chauffeur-bot in a peaked cap. Mr. Volt sat in the passenger seat.

146

"Isn't Patricia coming?" George asked, as the car swung out into the road.

"No, she's out with her friends tonight," Mr. Volt answered. "Now, don't disturb me, please. I'm playing Extreme Total Smash-Up on my MOD!"

Mr. Volt closed his eyes and settled back, and for the rest of the journey George heard him muttering, over and over again, "*Kaboom! Pow! Kersmash!*"

At TinkerTech, Volt led George to the warehouse on the first floor. Robots sat at conveyor belts, packaging up the MOD devices. More bots were placing the boxes onto pallets and loading them into a fleet of trucks.

"Here we are, George," Volt said. "Get packing!"

"But . . . it's all being done by robots," George objected. "Why do you need me?"

"You're an apprentice," Volt answered. "And apprentices do what they're told."

"Then why isn't Patricia doing it?"

Volt wagged a forefinger in George's face. "Be careful,

now. You want me to tell Professor Droid you refused to help?"

"All right, all right," George said. He could see there was no point in arguing.

"I have to go to my office," Volt announced. "To do some, ah, very important work. But I'll be watching you, okay?" He pointed to a security camera mounted on the wall. "So no funny business!"

As Volt strode away, George heard him repeating "Kaboom! Pow! Kersmash!" *Important work, huh?* George thought. *Yeah, right.*

He flopped onto the bench beside the conveyor belt at the end of a long line of robots packing boxes. If this was what it took to get his apprenticeship back on track, so be it. The conveyor belt was transporting empty boxes, and the robots were lowering the MOD devices inside them. Judging by his position in line, George saw it was his job to simply tape the boxes closed.

"Pretty exciting, huh?" he said to the robot at the bench next to him. The robot didn't answer. George guessed it didn't even have a speech program.

Watching the robots at work, George did some rough calculations in his head. By his estimate, the factory was packaging close to ten thousand MODs an hour. Mr. Volt's claim that 98 percent of the population would soon be wearing them didn't seem too far off the mark. *Almost every person in Terabyte Heights is wearing something designed by Micron.* The thought made George shiver.

Thirty minutes passed, but it felt like hours. The sun had set, and George wondered just how long he would have to stay here. He was starting to feel stiff. He got up to stretch his legs, and tried to fight the sense of injustice that was burning in his gut. Volt had put him to work here as a punishment, that was clear. Maybe Patricia had even suggested it. From day one of the apprenticeship, she and her dad had been out to get him. He ripped off another piece of tape and angrily applied it to a box. He'd *earned* this apprenticeship, through hard work, years of research, and even risking his life to save the town from destruction — but look where all that had gotten him. Patricia and people like her could get away with anything because of who their parents were. He stared defiantly at the camera mounted on the wall and wondered if Volt was really watching, or was too wrapped up in his game to notice.

Why did he have to have Mr. Volt as a mentor, anyway? It seemed like Volt's only goal was to keep George from doing anything useful. He and Jackbot could have been testing the MOD rigorously, properly analyzing it for flaws. Instead they were rushing to deliver a product that no one really understood. Now it was too late.

Or was it?

George looked at the robots loading the pallets onto trucks. By morning, the whole town would be connected to MODs. George had only a few hours, but if he could just get one into a lab and analyze it, at least that would put his mind at ease. And if he did find a problem, then there might be a way to stop the deliveries.

George glanced at the camera again. What if Volt *was* watching? If George left his post, his apprenticeship would be over, and he could say goodbye to a career in robotics. He imagined the disappointment on his uncle's face. *Head in the clouds, George. Always dreaming. Never focusing on the things that matter . . .*

"What do you think I should do?" he asked the packing-bot at his side.

The robot kept on packing.

"That settles it," said George.

Another MOD came along the belt toward him, but instead of taping the box, George snatched its contents

and slipped the device into his pocket. He left his seat and walked briskly out of the warehouse, toward the elevators. The doors opened at his approach.

"Hey there, good buddy," said the elevator. "Where to?"

"Testing facility, please," said George.

An hour later, George sat at a desk in the lab, his eyes weary from staring at the screen. With every minute that passed, he'd expected to hear a security alarm and Volt's voice over the intercom, asking where he was. But his luck had held. As far as he could tell, there was nothing suspicious about the MOD. At its top level, it was a standard user-friendly operating system. He'd linked it to a computer port, and the monitor in front of him displayed the device's menu on a large screen: image gallery, calendar function, digital encyclopedia, gaming, maps, music stations, newsfeed, photo library, radio broadcasts, social media links, weather reports . . . The list went on and on. George couldn't see a single thing wrong with any of it. He'd entered each of the

options and followed every branch of functionality. It all seemed perfectly innocent.

But what if the apps concealed something more sinister? There was really only one way to find out, and George had been avoiding it.

His throat went dry as he took the lenses from their sterile wrapper. They weighed next to nothing and looked like normal contact lenses. But there was as much computing power in a single lens as in a twenty-first century supercomputer.

He brought his fingertip up to his eye and slid the first lens into place. Once both lenses were in, he blinked. He couldn't feel them at all. And his vision wasn't affected in the slightest.

Next he put the earbud into place and gave it a double tap to switch it on.

There was a tiny, distant hum, and a small green light appeared in the corner of his left eye. He'd expected to feel something, but there was no sensation.

So, now I just think of what I want? Okay, I want to play Extreme Total Smash-Up!

Instantly, an image appeared in front of George's eyes. It looked like a big sandy arena, with massive cyborgs striding toward him from both sides. He could still see the desks and windows and computers of the testing lab in the background if he focused on them, but otherwise the image on the lens took priority. He seemed to be in the cabin of a monster truck, with a steering wheel in front of him. The cyborgs began firing blaster shots. George wanted to put the truck into gear — and found the gearstick was magically there at his side. He drove straight at the nearest cyborg and fired, and the cyborg exploded into pieces.

Not bad! George thought. *No wonder Volt likes it!*

But he couldn't spend the whole night playing games. *Give me the newsfeed.*

At once, the image in front of him was replaced by a picture of a smoking volcano on an island, and a newscaster talking in his ear about an eruption in the Pacific. It looked incredibly real, as if George was actually hovering over the scene.

Okay. Now give me the most recent news stories about Dr. Charles Micron.

The volcano disappeared, and a second later George saw the all-too-familiar scene of robots running wild in Terabyte Heights. The newscaster was explaining that these scenes were the result of Dr. Micron's trying to take over the city, but that his plan had failed and he was now wanted by the police. The story continued, but it was all old stuff that George already knew — after all, he'd been there. The MOD seemed harmless enough. Maybe his instincts about it had been wrong, after all.

George reached up to his ear to remove the MOD and his arm felt suddenly heavy.

A soothing voice that seemed to come from inside his own head spoke. *"Don't worry, everything's fine . . ."*

But it wasn't. George's vision blurred a little as he fought to lift his arm.

"Just relax," said the voice.

A warmth spread through his body, dulling his senses and making him feel light-headed. Somewhere in his mind he recognized the voice, but he couldn't think of the person's name. The lab was swimming before his eyes. Panic welled up in his chest.

I've got to take it off, he thought.

"No, no. Don't touch the MOD," said the voice, deep inside his brain. *"You'll be fine if you just leave it where it is. Everything will be all right . . ."*

George couldn't move his right arm at all. As soon as he tried to lift his left arm, it began to tremble with the effort. Then it sagged back down to his side.

George stumbled to his feet in terror. He caught a

glimpse of himself in the glass wall, his arms pinned to his side by some invisible force. He tried to shout for help, but his mouth wouldn't open. Something . . . someone . . . was controlling him.

"You're mine now," said the voice. *"All mine."* With that, George finally identified the voice.

Micron!

As the warm numbness continued to spread, George knew he only had seconds left before he'd be completely under the MOD's control. With all the energy he could still summon, he threw himself against the wall, smashing the side of his head against it. The force of the blow made him reel and fall to the floor, but it also popped the MOD out of his ear. The warmth began to fade immediately, leaving him feeling queasy and uncomfortable. He lay there, trying to catch his breath. And suddenly, everything made sense.

Micron was using the MOD as mind control!

The absent-minded driver. And that TinkerTech worker who had shoved him off the bridge. George would bet everything he owned that he had been wearing a MOD too. George was right. Micron had been after him all along.

And if Micron could access people's thoughts through the MOD, then George didn't have long before Mr. Volt—

"George Gearing," said Volt over the building-wide intercom, "I see you've left your post. Return to duty immediately."

Not a chance, thought George. *I still need to figure out how Micron is doing this!*

He grabbed the earbud and linked it to the computer once more. This time, George accessed the settings and disconnected the device unit from the TinkerTech server. Now his MOD would not receive any wireless signal.

Then George set the computer's scanner to analyze the input signal fields associated with the bud. As he had expected, now there was nothing on the normal frequencies. Curious, he expanded the search to detect other forms of electromagnetic radiation.

And there it was. George sat back, astonished, as he scanned the data on the screen.

He had terminated any incoming signal from the TinkerTech server, and now that those signals were gone, George was able to isolate a pulse of low-energy alpha waves still beaming right into the device. And alpha waves were associated particularly with brain operation in deep sleep. George shook his head in awe. Micron was burrowing right into his victims' innermost thoughts—and because the alpha waves had been concealed beneath the wireless signal, no one had any idea he was doing it.

George stared at the innocent-looking earpiece. *It's a weapon,* he thought. A weapon that makes people behave like robots. And soon, unless George stopped that shipment, Terabyte Heights would be full of new bots. Human ones.

Using a microscope and a pair of delicate tweezers, George opened up the bud and discovered a tiny red chip embedded within. *That must be the alpha wave receiver!* he thought. Gingerly, he used the tweezers to remove the receiver and close the MOD. He placed the device back in his ear and tapped to turn it back on. It started up with a beep, and George braced for Micron's voice—but it didn't come. Without the red chip, the MOD was harmless. Relieved, George took out his smartphone and punched the first number that was stored.

Anne answered at once. "George, is everything okay?"

"Listen, Anne, I've found out something. Something big."

"Where are you?"

"At TinkerTech. I've been looking into the MOD. It turns out Micron's planning to enslave the whole of Terabyte Heights using mind control."

There was a pause. "You realize how insane that sounds, right?" Anne finally said.

"Well, yeah. I guess I do."

"Good. Now that's out of the way—what do you want me to do?"

"Put your dad on the phone," said George. "No,

on second thought, I'll come over. Micron might be listening."

"Okay, but I'm warning you—my dad might not hear you out. He's been acting weirder and weirder since the party."

George swallowed hard. Droid was wearing a MOD. "Just stay safe," he said. "See you soon." He hung up.

George was about to leave the lab when he realized he could use the device to his advantage. He reconnected the MOD to the TinkerTech server. This way, he would have wireless access to the computing power of the MOD without worrying about Micron getting into his head. It might be useful, in a pinch. Still wearing the MOD device, George hurriedly left the lab and headed toward the elevator. It was seven floors down to the underground passage that led from TinkerTech to Anne's house. The transporter would have him there in minutes.

Just as he got to the elevator, he saw the OCD-bot standing there, blocking his path.

"No time to clean, get out of the way," said George. "Dusting can wait for another day."

But the robot remained where it was, looking down at George. "I am not here to clean."

George waited for it to complete the rhyme, but it didn't continue.

"Why aren't you rhyming?" asked George.

"Because I am not the OCD-bot," said the robot. "I am the Caretaker. And I have come to take care of you."

10

George turned and sprinted back to the lab.

"There's nowhere to run, George Gearing," said the Caretaker.

A red laser beam shot past George's ear and burned a hole in the wall ahead. George smelled singed hair. He ducked, reached for the door, and pushed through. He slammed it closed and rammed the bolt across it.

There was a moment of silence as George stared at the metal door.

A horrible whine swelled on the other side—and then, George heard a screeching crunch as the teeth of an electric saw bit through the metal panel right above his head.

"A little door can't stop me," said the cold voice of the

Caretaker over the din. "I'm going to get you, George."

Heart hammering, George looked around the lab for what he knew he wouldn't find—another way out.

Then, the whining of the saw stopped. A square piece of the door fell into the lab with a terrific bang, and through the hole George saw the Caretaker reach in with its pincer attachment to unlock the bolt.

George's mind raced.

"Ready or not, here I come!" said the robot, rolling into the lab.

George threw himself down behind the desk.

"Where are you, George?" cooed the Caretaker, his voice low and dangerous. "Am I getting warm?" George could see the beams from its red, flashing eyes pan across the walls and floor as it surveyed the room.

Maybe when it moves away from that door, I can make a break for it, George thought.

As if it were reading George's mind, the Caretaker picked up a heavy wooden desk, like it was a child's toy, and wedged it into the open doorway with a loud crunch.

"There you are!" said the Caretaker. George froze. "No way out now. *Tsk, tsk.* You've been a very bad boy, George. You've caused my master quite a bit of trouble." It waved its finger laser from side to side, just like George's school principal, Mrs. Qwerty, used to do.

It rolled down the aisle between the desks toward him.

"Hmm, which attachment shall I use?" the Caretaker said, weighing its options from only a few feet away. "The laser is fun, but it's very *clean*. Too clean. The drill, perhaps? I know—the sledgehammer!"

George dived for cover.

CRRRASSH!

A huge hammer smashed into the floor where George had been crouching just a microsecond before. But he was already running across the room.

"You're a quick one, aren't you," the Caretaker said. "Let's see if you can outrun my steam cleaner!"

George looked frantically for another exit. The Caretaker was smashing through desks, one at a time, and was almost on top of him. George's eyes landed

on a ventilation panel on a nearby wall. *The MOD!*
George thought. *The MOD could access a map for me!*
He squeezed his eyes shut and gave the command in his
mind. *Show me a map of the first-floor ventilation system
for the TinkerTech testing lab—NOW!* Just then a virtual
map of the lab, with all the ventilation ducts marked
in red, appeared right before George's eyes. If he could
only get to that panel . . .

The Caretaker stopped directly in front of him, his arm rotating. The hammerhead disappeared and was replaced by a shining black nozzle. "Steam cleaner in place," the Caretaker announced. "Temperature: two hundred and twelve degrees."

Boiling point, thought George, as the angry robot pointed the nozzle at his face.

George grabbed the nearest thing off the desk next to him, which happened to be a computer keyboard, and swiped it at the enormous bot. It knocked the steam-cleaning attachment straight off, and the boiling hot spray erupted like a geyser.

"Playing dirty, are we?" said the Caretaker. "You leave me no choice then: Perhaps you want the electric screwdriver? Or how about something messier?"

George dived for the panel on the wall.

Through the open slats, George could see a dark tunnel beyond, barely big enough for him to squeeze into. But the panel was held in place by screws at each corner. He tried to get his fingernails under the panel's edge, but he couldn't get a grip.

George heard a low whirring behind him, and he turned to see a deadly-looking circular saw spinning a few inches from his face.

"Say your prayers, George Gearing!" the Caretaker said. "No one can help you now."

It moved to strike George with the saw, and George ducked at the last second. The blade cut into the metal panel, tearing a hole in the center.

"Actually," George said, with a grin. "You just did!"

Wasting no time, George dug his fingers into the hole and yanked at the panel with all his strength. It came flying off the wall and smacked right into the Caretaker's head.

Not risking a look back, George scampered into the tunnel and didn't stop until he had reached a junction. He paused to catch his breath, and finally peered back to see the Caretaker jabbing its saw attachment uselessly into the ventilation shaft.

"You will not escape, George Gearing!" it shrieked. "I will take care of you!"

George raced down the ventilation duct. He studied

the map displayed before him by the MOD and checked the route. It was straightforward—a quick left at the junction and then a right to reach the central vertical maintenance shaft. There he would climb down a very long ladder that should drop him right in front of the shuttle to Droid's house. As he moved along, he tried to think of someone he could tell—someone who could warn the town about the MODs. He concentrated on accessing the MOD and thought, *Give me contact info for Wanda Vector at the* Terabyte Tablet. An instant later, her name, email address, and cell phone number appeared before his eyes.

Call Wanda Vector's cell phone number, he thought. He heard a ringing from the earpiece, and then:

"Hello?"

George tried to make himself sound more adult. "Wanda Vector?" he asked, his voice unnaturally low. Better she didn't know who he was. Even if Wanda Vector thought George was a hero, he wasn't sure she would be ready to listen to a kid.

"Yes. Who is this?"

169

"Listen to me very carefully," George said. "The MOD device is not safe. Dr. Micron is back, and he's planning to use the system to control the people who get connected. That means almost everyone in Terabyte Heights is in danger!"

There was a pause as Wanda took it all in. "How did you get this information?" she asked.

"You have to trust me!" George said. "Please! Run the story in the *Terabyte Tablet*. Put it on your website. Tell everyone as soon as you can!"

"Who is this?" the reported asked, sounding suspicious. "Your voice sounds familiar."

"No, you're mistaken," George said, panicking.

"Well, I need to know my source!"

"Just say it came from a TinkerTech insider!" George said, and ended the call. It was the truth, after all. He'd almost reached the bottom of the ladder and the shuttle. As he climbed through the belly of the building, he knew for a fact that no one was deeper inside TinkerTech than he was.

. . .

A few minutes later, George emerged from the shuttle at Professor Droid's mansion. Moonlight shone through the windows, and as George made his way to the front of the house, he narrowly avoided being seen by the butler-bot that was patrolling the halls. George stepped out into the large foyer, with its black and white tiled floor, huge crystal chandelier, and spiral staircase. He could hear raised voices coming from the second floor.

"Put it on!"

"No! Dad, stop it!"

"Anne—put it on *right now!*"

"Arf! Arfarfarf!"

George knew that sound. Sparky was protecting Anne. George sprinted up the stairs, following the sound of the voices to Anne's bedroom. Through the open door, George saw Professor Droid advancing on his daughter, holding out a MOD. Sparky was growling and snapping at his ankles.

"Just slip it in your ear and you'll understand!"

Anne was backed right up against the wall, holding

a chair out in front of her like a lion tamer. "Get back, Dad—don't come any closer!"

Her eyes widened in relief when she caught sight of George standing in the doorway. He put his finger to his lips, and Anne nodded slightly. "Don't you have it in another color?" Anne continued, trying to keep her father's attention focused on herself.

"Another color?" Droid said, confused. "Why? White goes with everything!"

With Droid distracted by Anne's question, George took the opportunity to sneak up behind him and pluck the MOD out of his ear.

Immediately, Droid staggered and had to hold himself up against Anne's dresser. "What's happening?" he said, with a hand to his head. "How did I get here?"

George threw the earpiece on the floor and crushed it under his heel.

"It's okay now, Dad," Anne said, taking her father by the arm. She led him to her bed, where he sat down heavily. "How do you feel?"

Sparky, seeing that the danger had passed, stopped growling and went to lick Droid's face with his silicon tongue. Anne's father stared blankly in front of him. "Like I just woke up from a terrible dream. I remember doing and saying awful things these past few days, but I didn't care. It was as if I had no control over my own body!"

"That's because you didn't," George said grimly. "Micron did."

"What?" said Droid.

"The MOD was Micron's brainchild. He planted alpha-wave receptors in the prototypes that allowed him to control the minds of anyone connected to the MOD system! Once everyone in town has one, they'll all be under his influence!"

"But wait—you're wearing one right now!" Anne said. "How do I know *you're* not a MOD zombie too?"

"I removed the receiver from this one," George explained. "It's the only Micron-free MOD. No zombies here, I promise."

"Whew," Anne said. "I really didn't feel like having to poke you with a chair, Robot Boy. Okay, so what do we do now?"

Before Anne or Professor Droid could answer, the television suddenly switched on. The three of them turned to see the handsome face of Dr. Charles Micron smiling back at them. Sparky growled and lunged for the screen, but Anne grabbed hold of him and held him close to shush him. Micron was wearing some kind of shining chrome helmet, its internal tech glowing from within with an eerie blue light. It made him look like a modern-day Roman soldier, ready for war.

"Good evening, George," Dr. Micron said. "I know you're watching. I put a little something special in dear old Droid's MOD so I could keep a close eye on him, and I know my connection to him has just been broken. I'm guessing you had something to do with that." He chuckled. "You have a very annoying habit of getting in my way, Mr. Gearing. I'd be happy to simply get rid of you once and for all, but first—you have something I need."

George frowned. "What could you possibly need from me?" he wondered aloud.

"I know you have it, because you never take it out of your pocket. If you did, I would have been able to steal it long before now."

George's eyes grew wide, and he slowly reached into his pocket and touched the marble.

"I know all about it, George. I saw it on my security-bot's film footage from that night at the junkyard," said Dr. Micron. "And if you don't give it to me, I can make some very unpleasant things happen. See this helmet I'm wearing? It allows me to control beta-testers connected to the MOD network. That's quite a few folks in town—including the lovely Wanda Vector." George's heart sank. His attempt to alert everyone in town had failed. "And by tomorrow," Micron continued, "it will be everyone. Would you like a little demonstration?"

The camera panned back to reveal that Dr. Micron was sitting on a desk in a plush office. There was a Terabyte Heights seal behind him.

"That's the mayor's office," said Professor Droid. "How did he . . ."

As the picture widened further, George saw that Cornelius Buffer, the mayor of Terabyte Heights, was standing right next to Micron, his face completely blank.

"Hey, Corny—do me a favor. Jump out the window," Dr. Micron said with delight. And without hesitation, the mayor opened the window behind him, swung his legs out, and jumped.

George gasped. "I can't believe it," he said hollowly. "You killed the mayor!"

"Oh, he's fine," Micron scoffed. "We're on the first floor. *Corny!*" A moment later, the mayor clambered back through the window to stand next to Micron. He must have fallen into a bush on the way down—there were leaves and twigs stuck in his hair.

"You see?" Micron exclaimed. "He'll do anything I say—*anything*. Now, if I don't get what I want, people in this town are going to start getting hurt, do you understand?" He leaned in toward the camera and the

smile dropped from his face. "Bring me that marble, George Gearing," Micron growled. "Bring it to the junkyard. Oh, and don't try to run. Anyone who's wearing a MOD has been ordered to stop you by any means necessary." He smiled again, his teeth fantastically white. "See you soon!"

The screen went blank.

"That sick, twisted . . ." Droid began, but when he tried to rise from the bed he swooned.

Anne put a hand on his shoulder. "Dad, you're in no shape to help. You've got to stay here."

Droid reluctantly tried to rest while George and Anne huddled near the door to talk. "What do I do?" George asked. He didn't want to surrender the marble. But the alternative was unthinkable.

"I don't get it—of all places, why does he want us to come to your uncle's junkyard?" Anne asked.

George slapped his forehead. "Of course—*he* must be Mr. Freezie! I thought that the whole buy-out was too good to be true. That's why Otto never met the buyer. Micron had to hire someone to do the deal for him because he couldn't risk being recognized! He must have known about the hatch we found and decided to buy the junkyard so he could get inside! That's why he wants the marble. Remember how it glowed when we got near it? I bet it's the key to opening that hatch door!"

"But we still don't know what's inside," said Anne.

"It has to be something to do with Project Mercury," said George. "And Micron will do anything to get it." He sighed. "But how are we going to stop him?"

"Wait!" Anne said. "I have an idea. Give me that MOD."

"Why?" asked George as he handed it over.

"Just play along, okay? We have a direct link to the mayor's office here, since Dad talks to him so much," Anne said, as she switched on her computer and pressed some keys. "Hold on. Just move over there, in front of the screen." George did as he was told. Anne got a baseball bat from inside her closet and then walked over to stand next to George, holding the bat in front of his chest.

The monitor lit up and there was Dr. Micron again. He peered at them in confusion, but then grinned. "Young Miss Droid, how good to see you! And it looks like you've captured our mutual friend!"

"Yes, sir," said Anne in an expressionless voice. She touched the MOD earpiece. "I received your order through my MOD. George managed to destroy my

dad's device, but he wasn't quick enough to get mine. He is my prisoner." George put on a scared face. "I will deliver him to you right away."

"That's a good girl," Dr. Micron said. "You see,

George? You think you're so smart, but you're no match for me." He reached out and cut off the connection.

"That was genius!" George exclaimed.

"Wasn't it?" Anne said. She turned to Sparky. "Listen, boy—I want you to stay here and protect Dad, okay? If anyone tries to put one of these little white things in his ear again, bite them!" Sparky wagged his tail and sat at attention at the foot of Anne's bed.

Anne turned back to George. "C'mon, let's go!"

"Wait," George said, stopping her. "What *is* the plan, exactly?"

Anne shrugged. "I have no idea," she said. "But if we're going to beat Micron again, we've got to face him together." She reached out her hand. "Partners?"

George grasped her hand and smiled. "Partners," he replied.

11

The Droids' smartcar drove them swiftly toward the junkyard. The night had turned dreary, and a misty rain fell all around them. The streetlights shone yellow in the gloom, and puddles glistened with reflected light. George stared out the window, lost in thought. Exhaustion was creeping up on him—but he pushed it away. He and Anne were Terabyte Heights' only hope. He would be able to sleep again only when Micron was behind bars for good.

"So, where's your trusty metal sidekick?" Anne asked, breaking the silence.

George sighed. "At home with Otto. He's probably forgotten I exist."

"Why would you say that?"

"He still thinks he's in love with Patricia's robot. I know I hurt his feelings, but he won't listen to reason. Between Jackbot's Romeo complex and Otto getting rich—it's like I hardly know them anymore."

Anne laid a hand on his shoulder. "C'mon, George. Don't write them off yet," she said.

"If you say so," George said uncertainly, and turned his gaze back at the window. A handful of people were walking through the streets. Some were scurrying along the sidewalk, rushing to get out of the rain, while others, who had the telltale white bud in their ear, shambled along aimlessly, their movements wooden and slow.

George nudged Anne. "Look at all the people already wearing the MOD! They look like they're in a trance."

Anne shuddered. "It'll be much worse if we don't stop Micron!"

"We won't let it happen," George said, trying to sound more confident than he felt.

The car slowed, then stopped. "Destination reached," it said.

George and Anne jumped out and faced the open gate of the junkyard. George took a deep breath. "Okay. We have to get that helmet away from Micron. If we disconnect him from the MOD system, we will disrupt the alpha waves that are controlling everyone in Terabyte Heights, and they should be free."

Anne rested her baseball bat on her shoulder. "Micron is expecting me to be under his control," she said. "So he won't be watching me that carefully—like he will with you. The first chance I get, I'll try to knock that stupid helmet off his head."

As soon as they passed through the gate, there was a burst of savage barking from inside. A pack of robot dogs ran out from the shadows and surrounded them.

They were huge, heavy-looking brutes, with long, narrow heads, yellow eyes, and pointed steel teeth like nails.

"You don't suppose these guys like playing fetch, do you?" Anne muttered.

"Only if we're the bait," George said, back pressed against the fence.

Suddenly, a bright light poured over them from above, and George had to shield his eyes. A loud *chop chop* sound filled the air, and George squinted up through his fingers to see a helicopter descending out of the night sky.

The helicopter set down noisily in the junkyard parking lot, and the wind of its whirring blades made Anne's hair whip around her face. Mayor Buffer jumped out first, and stood like a soldier at attention as Dr. Micron disembarked.

"So we meet again, Mr. Gearing!" Micron said in a cheery voice. His chrome helmet glistened under the lights of the helicopter. "So glad you could make it. Nothing like a baseball bat for making people see sense, is there?"

"She didn't leave me much choice," said George through gritted teeth.

"Well, time is precious!" Micron said. "Miss Droid, bring him over here. If he tries to make a break for it . . . stop him at all costs."

"Yes, Dr. Micron," replied Anne flatly.

The robot dogs loped along beside them as they followed Micron to the spot where George had found his parents' car. But the old blue Prodigy was gone. In fact, the entire pile of junk was gone—leaving only the metal hatch, shining ominously under the yard's spotlights.

And there, below the Mercury symbol that he had seen before, George saw a small hollow, the same shape and size as his father's marble.

"Exciting, isn't it?" Dr. Micron said, rubbing his hands together. "I knew for a long time, George, that your parents were doing secret research somewhere outside TinkerTech. It took me years to find it, but I got there in the end. Now, open the door."

George slipped a trembling hand into his pocket. The marble was warm to the touch. He pulled it out and saw that it was glowing again, pure blue and beautiful, like a shining star in the night. Looking at it, George was heartbroken. His parents had trusted their secret to him, and now he had failed them.

"I can't," George whispered.

"You *can,* and you *will,*" Micron growled. "Because if you don't, I have many clever ways to make you. Besides, it could be your last chance to see your parents' secret laboratory for yourself."

George snuck a look at Anne, who winked at him

when Micron wasn't looking. Anne was right. It wasn't over yet.

"Fine," George said, and walked to the hatch. Taking a deep breath, he placed the glowing marble into the hollow. It turned bright white. There was a low, melodic hum, and then the metal door slid slowly to the side, revealing a flight of metal stairs descending into total darkness.

"Splendid!" said Dr. Micron, snatching up the marble from its hollow. "You first, George. Miss Droid, you follow, and keep that bat handy, yes?"

His heart pounding, George slowly made his way down the stairway, feeling his way through the dark. Despite the danger he was in, he was tingling with curiosity. So this was where his parents had worked. He was about to learn the truth about Project Mercury!

It got colder as they descended, as if they were entering a walk-in freezer. George's footsteps clanked and echoed, in what he figured must a very large space all around them that they couldn't see. He reached the bottom of the stairs and Anne bumped into him. They stood there silently as Micron and the pack of robot dogs joined them, lit up by the marble that was glowing in Micron's hand. It made George's insides twist to see Micron holding the marble, but all that was washed away when the lights flickered on.

George blinked rapidly as his eyes adjusted to the wonder of his surroundings. He was right — the place was huge! The staircase they had descended was built against one wall of a large, industrial-looking workshop. Pieces of laboratory equipment were all around — tubes and coils and pumps and wheels and pipes and cables and screens and dials, and all of it began winking with multicolored lights. Everything was connected to everything else in a sort of haphazard, ramshackle way — wires trailed all over the floor, and George saw that several pieces of equipment were held together with duct tape. He grinned. This was just the sort of crazy, spontaneous, homemade setup he would have loved to construct himself. And then he saw them. Against one wall were two tall, oval-shaped pods that looked a bit like upright Egyptian sarcophagi, except that they were made of stainless steel. Etched across the front of both pods was the Mercury symbol he had seen before on the hatch.

George stole a glance at Anne and she raised her eyebrows, as if to say, *Wow.*

"Hmm," said Dr. Micron, kicking a box of loose wires out of his way. "Bit of a mess, isn't it? No matter. Just as long as it works."

"Welcome, George," said a computerized voice. "To the Mercury Lab."

"My parents built all this?" George said, his voice hushed.

"They did," Micron sneered. "All behind my back while they were my interns at TinkerTech. I had an idea that they were keeping secrets from me, but I could never figure out where they were conducting their research." Micron was by now seething with anger. "All I ever did was help them, and still they kept all this from me! They even destroyed their lab at TinkerTech just so I wouldn't have access to their findings. But I knew what they were

on to; we worked together at the beginning, until they cut me out. I couldn't get my hands on the research to find out exactly *how* they were doing it." He shook his head in disgust. "Your parents were just like Droid. Small-minded people who couldn't see the true potential for their discoveries—the chance at greatness!"

George felt the blood drain from his face. His parents must have eventually seen the kind of madman Micron really was. That must have been why they decided to keep their research safe from him. George fought the urge to throw himself at Micron and pummel him with his fists. "So that's why you killed them?" he snarled. "You made that car accident happen because they wouldn't—"

"Control yourself, boy," Micron muttered. "I didn't kill them. They brought their fates upon themselves. They were so determined to protect their precious Project Mercury, they were willing to give up their own lives for it. To go where they knew I could never reach them."

"I don't understand," said George. "What *is* Project Mercury?"

Dr. Micron's eyes brightened with excitement. "In a word, George: *power!* The kind of power that people have dreamed of for thousands of years!"

"Power to do *what?*" George demanded.

"The power to take matter—arrangements of atoms —and convert it to information. You know—ones and zeroes, computer data. And just like that, you could send that information anywhere in the world in an instant, and convert it back to atoms once it gets there."

George's eyes widened. "Wait—are you talking about teleportation? Like, I step in the pod here and then appear in a pod in China a second later, like an email?" He saw Anne's eyes widen in amazement.

"Obviously," said Dr. Micron.

"That would change the world," George said slowly. "You wouldn't need cars, or planes, or oil . . ."

Micron rolled his eyes. "That's just the beginning," he said. "You think too small, my boy! You can do more than just *send things*. You can *immortalize* them. If I could save my atomic data indefinitely, I could live forever. I could be a god." His eyes were shining, and with the glistening helmet on his head, and his square-jawed face set in an expression of complete determination, he looked like he might be a god. An angry one.

Out of the corner of his eye, George saw Anne twirl a finger at her head, as if to say "He's nuts." And she was right. No wonder his parents hadn't wanted Micron to know about Project Mercury. He was completely off his rocker. He wasn't just a criminal. He was criminally insane.

"Now, all those lovely plans depend on this thing actually *working* after all these years," Dr. Micron added. "So we'll have to do a little test. Now, I just need a guinea pig . . ." He looked around the room, and his eyes landed on Anne. "Ah! Miss Droid. You'll do quite nicely." He pointed to the sarcophagus against the wall. "Now, if you please — get into the pod!"

12

George swallowed hard. He looked at his friend and gave a tiny shake of his head. There was no telling what would happen to Anne if she got into the machine.

"Yes . . . Dr. Micron," she said, a slight tremor in her voice betraying her fear. But Micron was too distracted to notice.

George's heart was thumping in panic. If Anne refused to get into the pod, Micron would know that her MOD was a fake. But if she went in . . .

Anne began to walk slowly toward the pod.

Dr. Micron went over to the biggest computer in the room—which looked like it had parts of a combination washer-dryer and a vacuum cleaner attached—and set George's marble in a hollow on top of it before tap-

ping at the old-fashioned keyboard. The machine came alive with light and sound. "I'm entering coordinates to transport you from one pod to the other. Simple tele-portation. Fingers crossed, everyone! We may need to do a bit of fine-tuning."

"What do you mean, fine-tuning?" George said.

"You know, the usual," Micron said. "In the very early experiments, before your parents decided to keep all the research to themselves, I remember there being a few glitches in the system. We'd managed to convert living matter to data, no problem. But the other way around—making the data back into flesh and blood—that was trickier. Of course, your good old mom and dad didn't use humans for the tests, just mice. Some of them got a bit . . . scrambled. Paws where their ears should be, upside-down heads, that sort of thing. A few got turned inside out, I believe."

George fought back a wave of nausea.

Anne had reached the door of the pod, and she slowly pulled it open. She looked back at George, terrified.

"Wait!" George said.

"Hmm?" said Micron, fiddling with the controls.

"Let me do it!" said George. "I'll be the guinea pig. Leave Anne out of it—this has nothing to do with her."

Dr. Micron rose and gazed at George, impressed. "Well, well, well. Chivalry isn't dead, after all! You know, now that I think about it, there's a certain poetic justice in you being the one to go." He grinned. "So be it. Miss Droid—make way for George!"

Anne moved back. Her face was torn between relief and dread.

"Go on, George," Micron whispered in his ear. "Reap what your parents have sown."

As he passed Anne on his way to the pod, she and George shared a look. *No!* Anne mouthed.

With shaking breath, George pulled open the pod door and stepped in. The door swung shut, leaving him in the dark, with only a thin slit of light peeking through the crack in the door. His pulse was racing. All he could hope for was that his parents had perfected the design and that the device worked—that he wouldn't reappear in the other pod with his head on backwards or his skin inside out . . .

"Here we go!" Dr. Micron called over the noise of the machine. "In five, four, three, two—"

CRASH!

"What the—?" said Micron.

"George!" shouted a loud, angry voice. "Where are you?"

It can't be! George thought. He kicked at the pod door and it flew open.

It was. Standing at the top of the stairs to the lab was Uncle Otto, looking like a rampaging giant in his work overalls, brandishing a huge, black, iron wrench.

"I'm taking my nephew back, you lying scumbag!" shouted Otto, as he thundered down the stairs. "And my junkyard too!"

George's heart soared. He had never felt so happy to see his uncle in all his life.

"You've made a big mistake, Otto," Dr. Micron said, his voice tight with anger. "A very big mistake indeed."

"That's Mr. Fender to you, you crook!" shouted Otto. "Tricking me into selling my precious junkyard for a bunch of dirty money! And for what? So I can go and hobnob with a bunch of tech geeks who couldn't tell a spark plug from a carburetor if their lives depended on it? No! I'm getting my life back—and you're going to jail!"

"A fine speech, Mr. Fender," Dr. Micron said. "But you got that last bit very, very wrong. Dog-bots—attack!"

One of the huge dogs lunged at Otto. Without hesitation, he brought the wrench down on its metal skull with a clang. It was out cold. But there were too many for Otto to handle alone.

Suddenly—wielding a broken car antenna in front of him like a sword—Jackbot appeared at the top of the stairs. "Fear not, friends! The mighty Jackbot has come to save the day!" He leaped up onto the stair railing superhero-style, shouting, "En garde!"

"Jackbot!" George yelled. "You came!"

"Of course I did," Jackbot answered, hopping off the

stair rail onto the floor. "Do you really think I'd let you have all the fun?"

George grinned. Old Jackbot was back!

With a yell, Jackbot leaped onto the back of one of the dog-bots and started riding it like a bull in a rodeo. It wrenched its head around, trying to snap at Jackbot, but before it could make contact, Jackbot jammed his car antenna into the dog-bot's main power switch. The bot slumped to the ground. Jackbot raised his antenna in the air and yelled, "All for one and one for all!"

George saw his chance and launched himself across the room at Micron. He made a grab for the helmet, but Micron was too quick and caught George, pinning his arms behind his back. "I've got you now, Gearing!"

But Micron was so distracted by his struggle with George that he didn't see Otto rush forward and smash his wrench into the big computer. It exploded in a shower of steel and silicon, and the light and noise of the machine died.

"NO!" howled Micron. His grip on George loosened,

and George seized the chance to grab the helmet from his head.

"You're finished, Micron!" George said, holding the helmet high like a trophy. Micron roared and lunged for the helmet, but before he could wrench it from George's hands, an alarm sounded.

"Interference detected!" a computerized voice announced. "Containment procedure initiated. System will self-destruct in thirty seconds."

George looked up to see the steel door at the top of

the stairs begin to slowly slide shut. "Everybody out!" he shouted. "Now!"

Dr. Micron ran across the lab and went flying up the stairs first. Small explosions erupted from the machines in the lab, making them spark and catch fire. Black smoke filled the air.

George and Anne raced after Micron, with the door nearly halfway shut. That's when George spotted it. His blue marble, still resting on top of the main computer, where Micron had left it. "I've got to go back!" he yelled, but Anne grabbed his arm and pulled him up the stairs.

"There's no time!" she shouted. "You have to leave it!"

George swallowed hard and followed Anne through the door. "Wait—where's Jackbot and Uncle Otto?" George shouted in panic.

"We're right behind you, good buddy," Jackbot piped up.

George breathed a sigh of relief and charged through the opening in the steel door.

Back on the surface, George saw that Micron had *not*

escaped the junkyard. Mayor Buffer, now freed from the MOD's control, was struggling with him near the helicopter. George watched the mayor knock Micron to the ground with a right hook to the jaw. "*That's* for making me your little puppet!" he shouted. "You're going to prison, Dr. Micron, for a long, long time."

Micron lay in a heap on the ground, his crisp suit wrinkled and smudged with dirt. "I can't believe it," he muttered, his eyes wide with disbelief. "All my beautiful plans ruined by children, grease monkeys, and junkyard robots!"

George swelled with pride.

"We got him!" he turned to say to Otto, and then realized that Otto was still on the stairs, struggling madly with the last robot dog, which had its jaws clamped hard on his arm and was trying to pull him back into the lab. George saw the smoke and fire emerging from inside.

"Otto!" he cried. The door was more than halfway shut.

George crouched down, reached through the hatch door, and grabbed Otto's hand.

"Let go, boy!" Otto shouted through gritted teeth. "Save yourself!"

George shook his head. "I won't lose you too, Uncle Otto!" He pulled with all his strength, in a desperate tug-of-war with the dog-bot.

Jackbot caught George around the waist and pulled, and then Anne joined in too. The three of them dragged Otto up the last few stairs.

First his head was through, then one arm, and finally his body was clear of the door.

But the robot dog held tight to his other arm.

"OTTO!" George shouted.

The steel door closed as Otto's howls of pain cut through the air.

13

The sun shone brightly through the hospital window, onto the white sheets of Otto's bed, the unshaven bristles of his jaw, and the gleaming silver robotic arm that doctors had just spent the whole night attaching to his shoulder.

"How does it feel?" George asked. He was sitting at his uncle's bedside with Anne and Jackbot.

Otto clenched and unclenched the steel fingers. "I guess I'll get used to it," he said.

There was a short pause, during which Otto tried to lift a water pitcher with his new arm but lost his grip. The pitcher tipped and almost fell, but George grabbed it. "Let me, Uncle Otto." He poured the glass of water and put it in Otto's other hand.

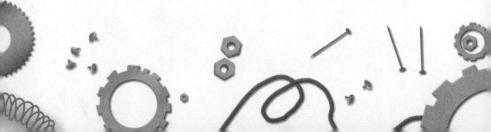

"Funny," said Otto, in a voice that suggested he couldn't actually see the funny side. "I never liked robots much, and now I'm half a robot myself!"

"Not half," Jackbot said. "An arm makes up approximately ten percent of a human body, Otto."

"Well, thanks a million, Mr. Know-It-All," said Otto, but George caught him trying to hide a smile.

"Otto," George said, lowering his gaze. "I don't think I've properly thanked you for saving me."

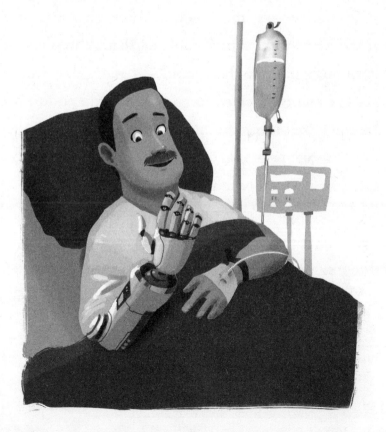

Otto waved his robot arm as if brushing the thanks away. "You're my nephew. You know I'd do anything for you, you big doofus."

"And you rescued me, too!" said Anne. "In fact, you saved the whole town."

Otto's cheeks flushed red. "It was nothing. Forget it."

There was something niggling at George's mind that he'd been wanting to ask. "Otto, how did you figure out that Micron was the one who bought the junkyard?"

Otto gazed out the window. "After what happened at the barbecue, I started realizing that all that money wasn't bringing me the happiness I thought it would. So, last night I decided to go to the yard and ask Mr. Freezie to sell it back to me. Your stubborn little robot wouldn't let me go alone, so he tagged along. We saw that hatch wide open, and we overheard what Micron was planning. Jackbot put two and two together, and well . . ." His voice trailed off. "We just had to do something, so I ran inside."

George smiled. "I'm so glad you did," he said, putting

a hand on his uncle's shoulder. "After all, what would Terabyte Heights be without Otto's Grotto?"

Otto blushed even deeper, then cleared his throat. "George, listen. I want to tell you something. I . . . I knew your parents had something hidden in the junkyard."

George gasped, then remembered how uncomfortable Otto had been when he had mentioned seeing the hatch hidden under his parents' old car. "But why didn't you tell me?" he asked.

Otto sighed. "I didn't know exactly what it was, but your folks made me swear that if anything happened to them, I'd keep you safe. That I'd only tell you about this stuff when the time was right. I just didn't think that time would come so soon." Otto met George's eyes. "George—I meant what I said that first day you went off to TinkerTech. You need to *be careful*, all right? Your mom and dad got into something bigger than they could handle when they were working there, and I'm pretty sure it got them killed. I just don't want the same thing to happen to you. Now you know the truth about all this—I can't help that. But can you promise me you'll stay out of trouble?"

"I promise," said George. "Anyway, all the stuff inside the lab's busted, and Micron's locked up. There's no more trouble to get into." George swallowed hard as he recalled having gone back into the lab that morning to see what was left after the self-destruct sequence had been completed. The secured hatch had been removed by paramedic-bots while they were rescuing Otto. Inside, the walls of the lab were blackened by fire, and the whole place smelled like melted rubber and burned metal. The machines were mangled and burned, but partially salvageable. George had already begun thinking of how he might rebuild them . . . but Otto didn't need to know that right now.

A robot nurse in a blue uniform bustled in, wheeling a cart full of medicines. George noticed her name badge—Nurse Linux. "Time for your medication, Mr. Fender!"

"Thanks," said Otto, crunching up the tablets the nurse gave him and swallowing them with water. "Hey, can I get attachments fitted on this thing? You know, like a wrench, or an adjustable screwdriver?"

"I believe you can," Nurse Linux said. "But you must speak to the doctor about that. Now, don't overtire yourself. Your friends must leave your room — visiting hours are over."

"Rest up, Otto," said George, moving to the door. "You'll be out of here in no time." Despite how grumpy Otto could be, George missed him. Being alone in the house was starting to get lonely, even though Jackbot and Mr. Egg, the cook-bot, were looking out for him.

"Feel better soon, Otto," said Anne.

Jackbot reached up with his pincer to touch the metal fingers on Otto's new robotic arm. George saw his uncle's eyes get watery for a moment before he barked, "All right, all right. Get out of here, you kids."

George smiled, and closed the door to Otto's room softly behind him.

George, Anne, and Jackbot stepped out the front doors of the hospital only to find themselves face-to-face with

Patricia Volt. She was carrying a bouquet of flowers, and Cookie was hovering by her side. "What are you doing here?" George asked her.

"My dad is recovering from MOD withdrawal," Patricia said, not meeting George's eyes. "Apparently he played one too many games of Extreme Total Smash-Up."

George looked down and saw Jackbot staring at Cookie with eyes filled with longing. Cookie looked back, beeped, and finally said, "Your exterior is dirty and covered in a millimeter of rust. I can remove the contamination with my buffer attachment . . . if you wish."

If George didn't know better, he would have thought he could hear Jackbot's battery compartment thumping in excitement. George sighed. "Well, Jackbot? What are you waiting for?"

Jackbot looked up at George, then back at Cookie.

"Thanks for the offer, Cookie," Jackbot said. "But maybe another time. Right now, my best friend needs me."

George's heart soared as Jackbot clamped his pincer around George's hand and led him away from the hospital.

Anne offered George and Jackbot a lift in the Droids' smartcar, and George was about to say yes when Jackbot interrupted. "Do you mind if we walk?" he said to Anne. "I'd like to talk to George."

"Sure thing," Anne said. "See you later!" She got in her car and it sped away.

George and Jackbot walked across the hospital grounds. It was a pleasant spring day, and George enjoyed the feel of the warm air on his face and the scent of flowers all around.

They came to a wooden bench under a tree, and Jackbot sat down on it. "Come sit with me for a second," Jackbot said. "I have something to tell you, George."

"What is it?" George asked, still standing.

"I've finally decrypted the Project Mercury file we downloaded from Dr. Micron's office," Jackbot said. "It was the most elaborate software protection I've ever seen —many passwords, all kinds of firewalls, everything you could imagine and more. I'm guessing it's the work of your parents. They must have wanted to make sure that Micron couldn't break in. But after a bit of work, yours truly was able to hack their code, of course." Jackbot sounded quite pleased with himself. "Anyway, the file— it's . . . quite a surprise. You'd better sit down, for this, George."

"What?" said George, suddenly nervous. He sat beside his friend on the bench. "What did you find?"

"Most of the files cover the design for the Project Mercury machine," said Jackbot. "But there's an additional design for your marble. Turns out it's not just a way into the lab, but also a holo-projector, protected by a voice code."

"A holo-projector?" asked George.

"Yes, and it contains a message," said Jackbot. "From your parents."

A wave of heavy sadness enveloped George. "But . . . I don't have the marble anymore. It burned up in the lab!"

"No, it didn't," Jackbot said. He reached into his chest compartment and took out the marble. "I picked it up as I was running for the door."

George gasped. He took the marble from Jackbot and held it in his hand, its comforting, familiar warmth filling him with relief. "Jackbot, you're amazing!"

"I know," said the robot. "But you made me, remember? So I guess that makes you pretty amazing too. Now—" Jackbot's voice got serious again. "Are you ready to see the message?"

George stared at the marble, his throat dry. "Yes, but —how do I activate it?"

"The files say there is a password," Jackbot said. "Something only you would know."

George frowned. "I have no idea what it could be."

"Think, George," said Jackbot. "There must be something you shared with them. Something private."

George racked his brain. Since the day his father had put the marble into his palm and closed his tiny fingers over it, George had carried the marble with him everywhere. "Keep this safe, Georgie Porgie," his father had said. "Keep it safe, for your good old dad."

"Porgie!" said George suddenly.

Jackbot cocked his head. "I'm sorry?"

"That's what they used to call me. After some nursery rhyme—*Georgie Porgie*."

Suddenly, there was a vibration in his hand. George looked down to see the surface of the marble swirling and shifting, as if it were mercury itself. George lowered it onto his lap, shielding it with his body in case anyone else could see. As the marble glowed white, two figures appeared above it, beamed there with rays of light. George's mouth uttered something between a gasp and a wail of shock. He was looking at his parents.

"Hi, George," said his father.

"If you're getting this message," his mother said, "then you've cracked the code, and you know all about Project Mercury."

"We knew you could do it," his dad said. "We're so proud of you. Now that you're old enough, you're ready to know the whole truth."

The whole truth? thought George in complete astonishment. *What do they mean?*

"We're not dead, George," said his mother.

George thought his heart had stopped.

"We're . . . in storage," continued his father. "To prevent Dr. Micron from getting his hands on us and the Project Mercury technology, we had to convert ourselves to binary data. Please. Do not trust him, George. Under any circumstances."

"Now listen carefully," said his mother. "You can

bring us back, George. With Project Mercury, it can be done. Depending on how long it's been since we disappeared, the machine may need a little tuning up—"

George thought of the smoking hulks in the Mercury Lab and swallowed hard.

"But you're a Gearing, George. And Gearings never give up," she finished.

"Once you locate our data," his father said seriously, "use the machine to convert us back to atoms."

"I know we're asking a lot of you, son," his mother said. "But we believe in you."

"We love you, George," said his dad. "No matter what happens, remember that."

And just like that they were gone. But their words echoed in George's heart. He stared at the marble, then at Jackbot, then back at the marble, speechless.

"I told you it was a surprise," said Jackbot.

JACKBOT
CONSTRUCTION DOCUMENT

V 1.203.41.206

MODEL NO. JB-012 7042

SCALE
10   30

PLAN No.1

FRONT

A

B

C

BRAIN SIMULATOR

OPTICAL RECEPTOR

NECK PLATE

SHOULDER JOINT

POWER CORE ACCESS HATCH

ELBOW JOINT

SUCTION CUP
MAX 250 LBS

KNEE JOINT
ROTATION LIMIT 180°

FOOT

15' 13'

36'

15'

9'

4'

3'

A

360°

ROTATION ORDER

d

n

$$\frac{d}{dx}\sin u = \cos u \frac{du}{dx}$$

$$\frac{d}{dx}\left(\frac{u}{v}\right) = \frac{(uv - w)}{v^2}$$

HEIGHT 36'
WEIGHT 100 LBS

-⊙- C-2656"
MODEL

JB-01

xxxx.12
2056   0

1   2   3